Good-bye, Billy Radish

by Gloria Skurzynski

Aladdin Paperbacks

Excerpt from "Smoke and Steel" by Carl Sandburg,
copyright © 1920 by Harcourt Brace Jovanovich, Inc.;
and renewed 1948 by Carl Sandburg, reprinted by
permission of the publisher.

First Aladdin Paperbacks edition October 1996
Copyright © 1992 by Gloria Skurzynski

Aladdin Paperbacks
An imprint of Simon & Schuster
Children's Publishing Division
1230 Avenue of the Americas
New York, NY 10020

Also available in a Simon & Schuster Books for Young Readers edition.

Printed and bound in the United States of America
10   9   8   7   6   5   4   3   2   1

The Library of Congress has cataloged the hardcover edition as follows:
Skurzynski, Gloria.
Good-bye, Billy Radish / by Gloria Skurzynski.—1st ed.
p.   cm.
Summary: In 1917, as the United States enters World War I,
ten-year-old Hank sees change all around him in his western
Pennsylvania steel mill town and feels his older Ukrainian
friend Billy drifting apart from him.
1. World War, 1914–1918—United States—Juvenile fiction.
[1. World War, 1914–1918—United States—Fiction.   2. Mills and
millwork—Fiction.   3. Friendship—Fiction.   4. Ukrainian
Americans—Fiction.   5. Pennsylvania—Fiction.]   I. Title.
II. Title: Good-bye, Billy Radish.   III. Title: Good-by, Billy Radish.
PZ7.S6287Go   1992
[Fic]—dc20   92-7577
ISBN 0-02-782921-9

ISBN 0-689-80443-1 (Aladdin pbk.)

For Serena and David Nolan, in memory of Sean Allen

ACKNOWLEDGMENTS

The author is grateful to George Yasko, who knows more about the Duquesne Steel Works than any other living person, and to Carol Yasko for reading this manuscript in its various metamorphoses. Thanks also to Lorraine Novak. She exemplifies the people of Duquesne—solid, spirited, and enduring. Here's to the city's second century.

—GS

A bar of steel—it is only
Smoke at the heart of it, smoke and the blood of a man.
A runner of fire ran in it, ran out, ran somewhere else,
And left—smoke and the blood of a man
And the finished steel, chilled and blue.
So fire runs in, runs out, runs somewhere else again,
And the bar of steel is a gun, a wheel, a nail, a shovel,
A rudder under the sea, a steering-gear in the sky;
And always dark in the heart and through it,
     Smoke and the blood of a man.
Pittsburgh, Youngstown, Gary—they make their steel
with men.

In the blood of men and the ink of chimneys
The smoke nights write their oaths:
Smoke into steel and blood into steel;
Homestead, Braddock, Birmingham, they make their
steel with men.
Smoke and blood is the mix of steel.

—CARL SANDBURG

JOIN THE
ARMY AIR SERVICE
BE AN AMERICAN EAGLE!

CONSULT YOUR LOCAL DRAFT BOARD. READ THE ILLUSTRATED
BOOKLET AT ANY RECRUITING OFFICE, OR WRITE TO THE CHIEF
SIGNAL OFFICER OF THE ARMY, WASHINGTON, D. C.

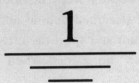

1

April 14, 1917

"Billy! Stop!" Hank yelled from the top of Center Street hill. "Stay right where you are. Don't move."

Obediently, Billy halted in midstride on the flight of stairs that descended from Chestnut Street to Center Street. "How come?" he called up.

" 'Cause I want you to watch me." About a hundred yards of Center Street separated them; a hundred yards of steep, downhill slope paved with yellow bricks. Hank ran down it often when he went to the store for his mother. No one ever ran *up* Center Street, not for more than a block or two, anyway. It was probably the steepest paved hill in western Pennsylvania.

Hank knotted the white silk scarf around his neck so that one end hung down to his knees, then threw the long part over his shoulder. "Watch this, Billy," he yelled. As he started to run, the heavy dinner pail he had to carry put him off balance, so he tucked it under his arm like a football. Faster and faster Hank ran, sprinting toward Billy, who waited on the wooden steps, not looking back to check how well the scarf streamed behind him, because to look back would slow him and spoil the effect.

"Did you see it?" he gasped when he reached Billy. "How'd it look?"

Billy knew exactly what he meant. "Just like in the picture," he answered. "Where'd you get it? Whose is it?"

"My brother Karl's."

The evening before, Hank and Billy had cut an artist's drawing from the newspaper—a picture showing an American pilot in the cockpit of his airplane somewhere over France, ready to fight the Huns, now that America had entered the Great War. The pilot wore goggles over his leather helmet, and a white silk scarf sailed behind him in the wind. After Hank thumbtacked the picture to his bedroom wall, both boys had sat admiring it for a long time.

"It's silk, like in the picture," Hank said, fingering the scarf. "Karl wears it when he gets dressed up to go to fancy dances."

Billy, too, stroked the silk, but only after he'd wiped his hand clean on his shirtfront. "Is Karl going to join up? Did you find out yet?" Billy asked.

"No, not yet." Hank hoped Billy would take that to mean he hadn't yet asked Karl. In reality, he had, and Karl had said no, he wasn't planning to join the Army Air Service or anything else, at least not yet, because for now his job in the mill was as important to the war effort as being a soldier or a flying ace in France. Steel was absolutely essential, Karl said, in this war that would make the world safe for democracy.

Past the bottom of Center Street, between Canaan Avenue and the river, steam rose in tall pillars of white against the gray daytime sky. Every night, flames from the Bessemer furnace set fire to the darkness above the Canaan Works of the Carnegie Steel Company. Night and day, all year long, the mill mixed iron ore and limestone and coal that came from inside the earth and turned them into steel beams and rods. And from those into rifles and cannons and shell casings and parts of airplanes that hovered over the earth. Airplanes that his brother Karl, at least for the time being, did not want to fly.

"America only declared war eight days ago," Hank said apologetically. It had happened on April 6, 1917, the Friday before Easter, a date their teacher said would live forever in the pride-filled hearts of all good American citizens.

"Yeah." Billy took out his handkerchief, unfolded it, put it carefully on the fourth step from the bottom, and sat on it. He was wearing his Sunday suit with the long pants that made Hank rigid with envy.

Hank's knickers—detested word—bulged just below his knees. Black stockings stretched from the bottoms of the knickers to the tops of his high-buttoned shoes. Boys' clothes! Billy, who'd turned thirteen in January, had already graduated to men's clothes because he was so much bigger than Hank—four and a half inches taller and thirty pounds heavier. Or maybe it was because Billy's parents weren't real Americans yet, and as Billy said, they didn't always know things—like that in America boys weren't supposed to wear long pants until they reached the age of fourteen. No one could blame Billy for not telling his parents that, since it allowed him to be the only boy in class who wore long pants.

Hank sat down beside him and put the heavy dinner pail on the step below—the third from the bottom of the wooden stairway. That was where he'd met Billy, almost four years earlier.

It was summer then. Seven-year-old Hank had sat alone at the halfway point of the long flight of wooden stairs that descended from Chestnut Street to Center Street hill below. Dank, soot-specked weeds grew through the worn boards. He'd pulled seed pods and thrown them into the air while he waited.

Every evening when the six o'clock whistle blew, Hank would run to sit at the middle of those forty wooden steps. From there he could see the day-turn men climb the hill. The hot, low sun that felt good on his bare legs shone straight into the eyes of the steelworkers returning home.

He could recognize his father the moment Hugo Kerner turned the corner from Canaan Avenue, but before running down to greet him, to take the dinner pail from his father's blackened fingers and carry it proudly home, Hank always waited until Hugo had climbed the hill halfway.

One especially hot August evening it occurred to him that the workmen creeping up the hill looked like ants:

stooped over, and black with grime from the mill. At that moment his father had rounded the corner. Hugo Kerner stopped, took off his cap, and wiped his forehead with a big blue handkerchief. Then he raised his eyes and took a deep breath, as though he needed to call up his strength for the long climb up Center Street.

Even from that distance Hank could see how worn-out his father looked. Hugo wasn't young; in the sun, his short gray hair had shone almost silver. Hank decided not to wait, but to run all the way to the bottom of the hill to carry his father's empty dinner pail and the newspaper Hugo always bought at the mill gate.

Hank jumped up to run, but he tripped. Tumbling the length of half the staircase, he scraped his legs as he fell until he caught himself against a worn riser, three steps from the bottom. A splinter as large and sharp as a jack-knife blade had broken off to stab him above the knee, making the flesh of his bare thigh rise up like dough lifted on a spoon.

"Ow! Ow! Ow!" Arms around his knees, he'd wailed, afraid to pull out the splinter because his swollen, bloody leg looked so ugly. If he went home, his mother would pour iodine on the wound, and iodine stung.

When he'd stopped wailing long enough to catch his breath, Hank had heard a noise under the steps. One bare leg emerged, then another. A boy he didn't recognize had been sitting there in the dirt, in the weeds, underneath the stairs. Maybe he'd been looking for pennies that had fallen through the spaces. Hank did that sometimes.

"Who are you and what do you want?" Hank had

demanded in an angry voice, ashamed he'd been caught crying.

When the boy didn't answer, Hank had asked, "What's the matter with you? Can't you talk?" Even though the boy was bigger and older than Hank, he didn't look the least bit mean.

The boy said something Hank didn't understand.

"You're a foreigner," Hank accused. "You can't speak American."

Gently, the boy pulled the splinter from Hank's leg, then dabbed the cut with a clean, folded handkerchief.

"You're getting the hankie all bloody!" Hank had yelled. "Your mom's gonna holler at you."

Not attempting to answer, the boy shook out the handkerchief and tied it around Hank's leg. Hank scrambled to his feet. "What's your name? Me—Henry Kerner," he said loudly, pointing to his chest. "Only, call me Hank instead of Henry, 'cause I like it better. Who you?" He pointed to the boy.

"Bazyli Radichevych," the boy had answered.

"That's too hard," Hank told him, but the boy just repeated, "Bazyli Radichevych."

"No. Listen to this," Hank said. "Billy Radish. You say it. Billy Radish."

The boy considered the matter, his expression serious. Then he nodded. "Bee-lee Rah-doosh," he said.

"No. Like this. Bill-ee Rad-ish."

"Bee-lee Rah-dish."

"That's better. Now say this." Hank pointed to the red gore trickling down his leg. "Blood!"

6

"Blahd! Blahd!"

"You're a dumb Hunkie."

"You dom Hawnkie."

Hank laughed. "Not me . . . you!"

"Nommee. You!" Billy laughed, too, his soft upper lip pulling back to show that he already had his second teeth in the front, both top and bottom, where Hank had only empty spaces.

By the time Hank remembered to look for his father, Hugo Kerner and all the rest of the steelworkers had already reached the top of the hill, where Hugo would trudge up Pine Alley to his backyard. Their lot stretched from Center Street in front to Pine Alley in the back.

"Well, come on," Hank had said, gesturing for Billy to follow. "My pop's already gone home, so I'll take you with me and show you where I live. Maybe I'll teach you how to talk in American, if you're not too dumb."

"Dom. Dom Hawnkie," Billy repeated as he followed Hank up the street.

Starting that evening, the two boys played school daily—Hank in the role of a bossy teacher and Billy a meek but willing pupil. Nine-year-old Billy knew how to do arithmetic problems and he worked hard to learn English; seven-year-old Hank was smart enough that he could skip second grade. When school began after Labor Day, the boys found, to their delight, that they'd been put in the same third-grade classroom. They became inseparable.

"We do not use nicknames in this class," Miss Pate, the teacher, had said sternly. "Billy Radish is not your real name." But even for her, Bazyli Radichevych was quite a mouthful. Before long she called him Billy Radish, too, just like Hank and everyone else did.

Now, sitting on the step beside Hank, Billy asked, "What's the dinner pail for?"

"Karl had to go to work early, before my mom had it packed for him. I have to take it to him in the mill," Hank said, grimacing. "I want you to go with me."

Billy shook his head. "Hear that bell?" he asked.

From the top of Oak Street, a bell in the spire of the Russian Orthodox church had begun to ring. "Yeah, I hear it. Sounds like somebody died," Hank said. "So what?"

Every time a member of the Russian Orthodox church died, the bell tolled one stroke for each year of the dead person's age. When they were smaller, Billy and Hank had always tried to count the peals, making a game of it: If the dead person were quite elderly, they'd get all the way up to sixty or seventy before losing count. They hardly ever did that anymore.

"No, no one died," Billy was saying. "That's not the death bell; it's a different one—can't you tell? It means I have to go to church for the blessing of Easter eggs. I'm wearing my church suit, see?"

"Today isn't Sunday. It's Saturday."

"I know. Holy Saturday. Our Easter's tomorrow."

"You people ought to have your Easter when everybody else does," Hank protested. "The real Easter was last week." Each religious holiday seemed to be celebrated a week or more late in the Russian Orthodox church, which Billy's family attended because there wasn't a Ukrainian

8

church in the town of Canaan. "Anyway, blessing Easter eggs sounds like a dumb waste of time. Who cares if they're blessed? Why can't you just skip it?"

"It's not dumb," Billy said. "Easter eggs are important."

"But I want you to go to the mill with me!"

Billy squeezed Hank's biceps, or what Hank liked to think of as his biceps, although there wasn't much muscle to squeeze in his upper arm. "It'll be all right, Hank," he said. "Maybe you won't have to go inside the mill. Maybe you can just give the dinner pail to the guard at the gate. It'll be all right. Don't worry."

But the mill always worried Hank.

2

The mill m de noises like a giant giving birth—shrieks, screeches, whines, clangs, blasts of locomotive whistles, rumbles of machinery, the groan of cranes, the roar of coal unloaded into piles higher than houses. In Hank's hand, the dinner pail grew heavy as an albatross.

They'd been studying *The Rime of the Ancient Mariner* in reading class. "If someone tied a dead bird around my neck, I'd just take it off," Hank had told Billy after school. "That Ancient Mariner was stupid to leave it on."

But certain things couldn't be cast aside so easily. The steel mill had frightened Hank since he was four years old. It began on the afternoon when Mayo Culley, their next-door neighbor, had lifted little Henry Kerner (he wasn't yet called Hank) onto his lap with his left arm. Mayo's

11

right hand was useless; it lay clawlike on his right knee. The hand looked dead—discolored, ropy with scars, mangled and ugly.

When Hank had begun to cry, Mayo had asked, "Is it the hand that's botherin' you, then, lad? Don't be afraid of it. Here, touch it, so you'll know it can't hurt you."

Hank had screamed all the louder until his father carried him inside. "Don't fret like that," Hugo had scolded. "You'll make Mr. Culley feel bad. He can't help it—it happened in a mill accident."

Not long after that, Hank had gone down-street with his father on a winter afternoon. Snow had fallen, but soot had fallen as fast as the snow, blackening it. His father needed to go inside the bank, Hank remembered, to pay the water bill. Maybe he'd never taken the little boy to the bank before, because it was the first time Hank had noticed the two beggars seated on the pavement outside Canaan's First National Bank.

He was the right height to stare directly into the eyes of the two ragged men, except that one of them had no eyes. The man held a tin cup in one hand and half a dozen pencils in the other. Hugo had dropped a nickel into the cup; the man heard it fall and said, "Bless you, sir." Hugo didn't take a pencil.

The other man sat on a square wooden platform with skate wheels nailed to the bottom. As Hank watched, horrified, the man wheeled himself around the corner, pushing the platform with his knuckles because he had no legs.

"Mill accidents," Hugo said again. "Both of them."

12

Hank had clung tightly to his father's sturdy legs, and had buried his head against the thick wool of Hugo's trousers until Hugo pried him loose at the bank door. For months afterward Hank had awakened screaming from nightmares about eyeless, legless, mutilated men who'd been swallowed by a huge shrieking furnace.

Now he clutched Karl's dinner pail and stood unmoving in front of the mill gate.

"Why do I have to take this thing to Karl?" he'd demanded of his mother an hour earlier.

"Who else do you expect me to send?" she'd asked him. "Both your father and Karl are already at work, so that leaves you. I don't know why you always make such a fuss about the mill. It won't be long before you're working there yourself."

"Not me!" Hank had insisted. "Never!"

"Of course you will," his mother had answered. "Every man and boy in Canaan ends up in the mill sooner or later."

Through the open door of the guardhouse, the guard stared curiously at Hank, who was pulling on the ends of the silk scarf to make them even. Then he stuffed the silk through the neck of his shirt, hoping the bulkiness of the brown sweater he was wearing would hide the scarf's outline. He hadn't bothered to ask Karl if he could wear it; he'd just taken it out of Karl's top drawer and tucked it inside his sweater until he was out of the house.

"Where's Number One Open Hearth?" he asked the guard.

"What you want to know for? We can't let just everyone come in here, you know. There's a war going on." The man didn't sound unfriendly; Hank knew he was just following procedures.

"My brother works at Number One Open Hearth. His name's Karl Kerner, and I have to take him this dinner pail." Hank hoped the guard would tell him he was too young to enter the mill, or that because of wartime security, they had messengers to deliver dinner pails to the steelworkers inside, and that he, the guard, would take charge of the dinner pail and Hank could go home. But that didn't happen.

"See the dinkey engine over there?" the guard asked. "That little locomotive pulling a load of ingots? Number One Open Hearth is right behind that. Wait till the engine gets past, then run like the devil before the next one comes."

The ingots, standing upright like enormous scorched dominoes, still glowed orange with heat. Hank backed away and waited until the last ingot-bearing car had passed him, then he sprinted across the tracks so fast that the lid of the dinner pail clattered like artillery.

Number One Open Hearth was a high, steel-sided building about twenty times as big as a barn. Inside, six huge furnaces stood side by side, identical as row houses on a street. Hank walked past the first furnace, which stood cold and idle, waiting to be relined with new bricks. At the second, three men lounged while the batch of molten steel—sixty tons of it in just that one furnace—heated to the proper temperature. Open-hearth work went in fits and starts, Karl had told Hank: Charge the furnace with scrap steel, ore, and limestone, heat the charge, wait while it got hot enough, stir, wait, test, wait, add molten iron, wait, test, wait, then, finally, tap the furnace, letting the newly made steel run out in a stream while the slag ran off.

He found his brother Karl in front of the third furnace. The boss, Matt Gable, relaxed on a stool next to Karl. Hank had never met Matt Gable, yet he recognized him from Karl's description—middle-aged, growing soft in the body, but with still-powerful shoulders toughened from years of stirring molten steel. Lately, though, Matt had allowed Karl to do most of the stirring.

As Hank watched, Karl pushed a long steel rod through one of the furnace doors. The reflection from the inside heat lit Karl's cheeks; the planes of his face changed from black shadow to orange glow. He stirred and prodded and explored the furnace bottom with the bar, feeling for un-melted lumps of metal, thrusting his body forward to in-crease his strength, growing wet from exertion until circles of sweat darkened his work shirt.

Hank clutched the handle of the dinner pail, not calling out because the distraction might put Karl in danger. With the furnace door open, nothing at all stood between Karl and that three thousand-degree batch of leaping, boiling, melting steel-in-the-making. Yet Karl grinned as he worked, obviously enjoying what he was doing. His nim-bleness and skill filled Hank with pride. That was his big brother, there—that tall, handsome twenty-year-old man whose job was as dangerous and important as any Amer-ican pilot's flights over the German lines. Karl was just as much of a war hero as an American flying ace.

"There! That baby's done," Karl said after the furnace door closed. Then he noticed Hank.

"Hank! How long have you been standing there?" he exclaimed, looking pleased. "Did you see me rabbling the furnace just now?"

"Yeah, I saw you. Here's your pail," Hank said, holding it out to him. "I waited till you were finished with the furnace."

"Furnace work is never finished," Karl answered, sounding proud of it. "Keeps me on my toes." He laughed then, and turned to the foreman. "Hey, Matt, this is my kid brother, Hank."

"Well, son of a gun!" Matt bellowed. "Shake, kid!" His huge, blackened paw of a hand swallowed Hank's in a crushing handshake. "He don't look nothin' at all like you, Karl. Not one bit."

That was true. Hank took after their mother—short and blond. The other two children in the Kerner family, Karl and Kathleen, were tall, slim, and dark-haired. And grown-up. Kathleen was married, and Karl was going to be.

Matt grinned. "You must keep pushin' this kid away from the table without lettin' him get enough to eat, Karl. He's a skinny little runt, ain't he?"

"He'll grow," Karl said, tightening his arm around Hank's shoulder. "In a couple more years he'll shoot up."

Hank thought Matt Gable should have been pushed away from the table a whole lot sooner. His round belly pulled gaps between the buttons of his grimy undershirt, and a roll of fat beneath his chin made his neck hard to find.

"Listen, Matt, as long as Hank's here, how about if he sticks around awhile? Is that okay with you?" Karl asked.

"Sure. Set him somewhere out of harm's way. He can watch the fireworks."

Hank had planned to deliver the dinner pail and get out of there as fast as possible, but. . . . "What fireworks?"

"Hot metal'll get poured into the furnace in a few minutes," Karl explained. "It's a terrific thing to watch! Like the Fourth of July, only better, even. Really wild!" He smiled at Hank. "But not too scary."

The sight of Karl pushing the rod through the furnace door had been scary enough, but Hank couldn't admit that to his big brother. Anyway, he'd sort of liked seeing Karl poke around the insides of the furnace—like Vulcan, a god of flames Hank had read about in a library book. "Where should I stand to get out of the way?" he asked.

Karl looked around. A piece of machinery the size of a boxcar stood on railroad tracks in front of the next furnace. "Over there by the charging machine," he answered. "Before you go, though, look above you." He turned Hank by the shoulders and pointed to the high ceiling where steel girders crisscrossed. "See that great big ladle coming along on the overhead crane? It'll dump tons of melted iron into our furnace. Slick as a whistle, the crane operator will stop the ladle right in front of furnace three—that's ours," Karl said. "Then he'll tilt the ladle, and all that molten iron's going to pour through a trough into the charging door of the furnace. That's the fireworks Matt was talking about, 'cause it sparks like crazy. It's great!"

Hank moved back to lean against one of the boxes of

limestone next to the charging machine. The box rested on a buggy; the buggy's wheels stood on a narrow-gauge railroad track.

"Look how sweet that crane operator handles that baby!" Karl cried out. "Just think, Hank, one man moving a great big ladle full of all that molten iron, and he stops it right on a dime. Maybe when you get bigger, you can learn to be a crane operator."

"Maybe," Hank answered, but inside he was shouting, No, not me; anyone would have to be crazy to work in here with all this dangerous stuff.

The ladle had stopped. With a clang, the charging door on the furnace opened. Matt Gable raised his hand, signaling the overhead-crane operator to tilt the ladle toward the trough.

The pour began, making sparks fly like a swarm of angry golden bees around the thick, fiery stream of molten iron cascading into the open-hearth furnace. It looked like an enormous, blazing hell. Everything was giant-size, super-heated, loud, noisy, fearsome. Hank stared at his big brother, who seemed incredibly pleased by the whole flaming scene.

"How do you like *that*?" Karl asked, grinning and elbowing Hank. "Fantastic, huh?" but when he turned back to look at the ladle, his expression changed. "Uh-oh!" Karl didn't even say it loudly.

Before Hank could understand what was happening, Karl leaped at him and threw him backward into the box of limestone. It hurt! Limestone gouged his back. Karl's body was on top of him so that Hank couldn't see anything, but there was a rush of sound unlike anything he'd ever heard before, then a tremendous clatter, and the ground shook beneath the buggy that held the box of limestone the brothers lay in.

"What . . . !" As he tried to fight his way clear of Karl's body, heat seared him. Rising to his knees, Hank saw molten iron swirl around the wheels of the buggy, filling the spaces between the narrow-gauge tracks. Glare nearly blinded him so that he couldn't see much, but he noticed Matt Gable.

Matt was on his hands and knees on the floor of the open hearth, in a pool of molten iron. He seemed to be melting.

"Don't look!" Karl yelled, forcing Hank's head down. "Stay still! They'll get us out of here pretty soon."

But Hank wanted to know why Matt was melting, and why Karl kept pushing Hank's face into the limestone. "What happened?" he sputtered, because granules of limestone had gotten into his mouth.

"Don't look! A lug broke off the side of the ladle. It fell and spilled. . . . Oh God! Stay down, Hank!"

Hank didn't fight; he let himself be pressed against the limestone because he was gagging. What he'd seen was true, then. Matt Gable really had fused into a pool of molten iron. If he'd melted that way, he must be dead.

"We'll be all right," Karl kept saying. "Just don't move till they come for us. Don't be afraid. I'm here with you. But don't move, and for God's sake, don't look!"

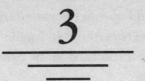

3

April 16, 1917

At eight o'clock Monday morning Billy knocked on the Kerners' back door.

"I'm not going to school," Hank said, opening the door no more than three inches.

"I figured you wouldn't. Let me in. I brought you something."

Hank let Billy slip through and asked, "What? What'd you bring me?"

"An Easter egg."

"What do I want with an Easter egg?"

Carefully, Billy pulled an egg from his jacket pocket. "It takes a long time to make Ukrainian eggs. My sister started this one for you right after we heard what happened in the mill. She stayed up till midnight Saturday night working on it." He opened his hand.

Jewellike, the egg lay on Billy's palm. Red, black, yellow, and blue, it was etched with tiny triangles and stars and crosses. "My mother says as long as Ukrainian women make eggs like this, the evil monster will stay chained up."

"What monster?" Hank touched the egg with his forefinger. Why would anyone, he wondered, spend all those hours working on something so fragile? If he dropped the egg, or squeezed it too hard in his hand, it would all have been for nothing.

"The monster who will eat everybody in the world if our women don't make enough of these *pysanky*," Billy answered. "If they make a lot, the monster can't move. If they don't make enough, his chains get loose and evil spreads."

"That's a fairy tale," Hank said. He wished he'd had the egg on Saturday before Matt Gable got killed, though.

Billy shrugged. "Maybe it is, maybe it isn't. I better go now. I'll tell the teacher why you're not coming today. Will you go to school tomorrow?"

Hank hung his head. "I guess so. The funeral's this afternoon."

"Yeah. So I'll stop by tomorrow morning, like always."

Hank put the egg in a teacup and set it on the kitchen table. Although he realized Billy had brought the egg to show the sympathy of the Radichevych family, he could barely mutter a "thanks." To say more would be risky, since Hank's own shell was close to cracking. He watched Billy walk all the way to the back gate before he closed the door.

"Mom," he yelled, and ran through the house to find her. His father and brother had gone to work but would be home in time to clean up for Matt's funeral. "Mom, are you upstairs?" Bounding up the steps, he found his mother in her room, making the bed.

"I can't wear these knickers to the funeral," he declared. "I just can't! You have to take me down-street and buy me some long pants right now."

"Oh I do, do I?" Maggie Rose Kerner snapped a sheet till it billowed. "Silly me—I thought you were too young for long trousers."

"Billy wears long pants and he's in the same grade as I am!"

"Billy's bigger and older."

"I don't care!" In a minute Hank was going to cry. He'd hidden himself in his room most of the day yesterday so he could cry without being seen. Even now the tears were so close to his eyelids that only by shouting and being angry could he hold them back.

"Everyone's going to stare at me in that church," he said. They'd all know that he was the boy who'd seen Matt die, and maybe if he hadn't been there Karl could have saved Matt instead. "If I have to wear knickers, I won't go!"

"You have to go. It's the decent thing to do since you. . . ." Maggie Rose studied him, her expression growing softer. Like Hank, she was short in stature, but while he was thin, his mother was sturdy; when he heard the expression "sturdy Irish stock," he thought it referred to his mother's shape. Her hair had once been as yellow as Hank's. Lately, enough white had spread through the yellow to make it creamy amber, and before long it would resemble ivory. She was forty-four, eight years younger

23

than her husband, and she had borne five children. Three of them still lived.

"All right, Hank," she said, "let me finish the beds and put on my hat, and we'll go down-street to Levine's Men's Clothing."

He hadn't expected his mother to give in; it gave him nothing to rage against. Blinking his eyes against the tears, Hank ran to his room, threw himself on his bed, and covered his head with the pillow. Instantly he pulled the pillow off his head and flung it across the room. When he covered his head that way—in fact, every time he closed his eyes—he saw the flowing molten iron and Matt Gable sinking into it. And heard the horrible sizzling sound like bacon frying in a skillet, but a hundred times louder. And smelled the charred-flesh stench that made him want to vomit all over again. And felt the mill closing in around him.

"They have to be finished in two hours," Maggie Rose told Mr. Levine.

"They will be, Mrs. Kerner. But think about this—one pair trousers costs your three dollars, including I'll shorten the cuffs. For ten dollars I'll fit him in a whole suit with two pair pants, because with a suit the pants get altered free." Mr. Levine had already pulled a boy's jacket off a hanger. "Try this on, Hank," he said.

Hank looked at his mother for guidance. Maggie Rose hesitated just long enough for Mr. Levine to slip a sleeve over Hank's arm, then shrug him into the coat.

"See? Big enough he'll get two years wear, maybe three. The pants we'll cuff one pair long, for today, and the other pair I'll make knickers like he always wears."

Maggie Rose cleared her throat. "Ten dollars for everything?" she asked.

Mr. Levine tilted his head as if to reconsider. "My wife says I shouldn't give such bargains or we'll finish our days in the poorhouse. But the Kerners are good customers—so go ahead. Take! I won't tell my wife."

"Hank's really too young for long trousers. . . ."

"Feel this material, Mrs. Kerner. Good serge, good color—navy blue won't show the soot."

"The trousers can be cuffed by noon? The funeral's at one o'clock."

"Mrs. Kerner, did you ever know Levine to promise what he couldn't deliver?"

Hank looked at himself in the narrow mirror. The legs of the blue serge pants had been folded up eight whole inches, and still they draped over his instep.

Wearing long pants, Billy Radish could be mistaken for a short man. In Canaan there were a lot of short men whose growth had been stunted because they'd nearly starved as children in Europe. Hank just looked like a boy wearing long pants before he was old enough.

"I guess he really could use a new suit," Maggie Rose decided. "Since it's such a good buy."

Inside the church door, Hank looked around for a holy water font, but couldn't find one. He followed his father to the center aisle and was about to genuflect until Karl, behind him, yanked him up by the collar of the new suit jacket. "They don't do that here," Karl whispered.

It was the first time Hank had been in a church other than his own Catholic church. This one seemed very plain:

no votive candles, no murals showing winged angels and robed saints, no statues of the Blessed Virgin—in fact, no statues at all. In the pew his father nudged him toward, there was no kneeler, either. How could he kneel to say a prayer for Matt Gable's soul?

"Just sit down and keep still," his father told him softly as Hugo himself settled his bulk on the wooden pew. Hank pressed so close he could feel the outline of his father's pipe, which Hugo carried inside his coat pocket.

At first Hank kept his eyes lowered, certain that everyone was staring at him. Wedged so tightly between his stout father and his tall brother, after a while he felt less noticeable. He began to glance around. The Presbyterian church looked crowded beyond capacity. News of the terrible way Matt had died had filled many people with pity and others with curiosity.

No one had been able to reach Karl or Hank or what remained of Matt until the spilled iron had cooled sufficiently. All that time the two brothers had lain inside the box of limestone on the buggy resting on the railroad tracks, with Karl forbidding Hank to look toward the lump of burned flesh that had once been Matt Gable. Karl had covered Hank's head with his shirt when the rescuers came to lead them past Matt's body. Later, after the iron cooled completely, mill workers had sawed around Matt and pried him from the platform along with the solidified iron, fused to him like the base of a statue.

Encased as he was in an iron shroud, it had been impossible to separate Matt from the metal, so they'd put everything into a closed coffin. The iron made it so heavy that ten pallbearers would be needed to carry it, Hank's father had heard.

The rumor proved to be true. The sound of shuffling feet made Hank turn to watch the casket being carried in. The ten men sweated, moving awkwardly because it was hard to fit ten people around a single casket. After they set it down, the minister began to speak.

"Matthew Gable," he stated, "is the first man from Canaan to die in this great war. Yes, you heard me right—Matthew gave his life for his country. He died making steel to forge weapons and build ships that will carry our brave American soldiers overseas to fight an enemy that wants to destroy the world! And so I say to you, Matt Gable died a hero's death just as sure as if he'd been shot in the trenches. We are sorry that our friend Matthew had to die. But he died for a great and glorious cause!"

Hank sat up straighter. He'd never thought about Matt being a hero. Matt hadn't actually *done* anything—he'd just been standing in the wrong place when the ladle broke. But the minister said that made him a hero, and many people in the pews were nodding in agreement.

If you had to die, Hank thought, it was probably a good thing to die as a hero. Walking to the funeral, he'd finally found the courage to ask Karl if Matt might have been saved, if only Hank hadn't been in the way.

"No," Karl had answered. "Absolutely not. Matt was a big man—there's no way I could have lifted him." Then Karl had taken Hank by the chin and forced him to look up, into his eyes. "You were standing right next to the charging box where the spill couldn't reach, and I could dump you in because you're light. Do you understand? I couldn't have saved Matt."

"Promise?" Hank had whispered.

"I swear to God! It's the truth."

As a pump organ put forth tremulous notes, the people began to sing "For All the Saints Who from Their Labors Rest." It was a plain kind of hymn, Hank thought. The people around him looked plain and sober and grim. In Hank's church, people knelt to finger rosary beads as their lips moved in quiet prayer, and the priest's voice alternated with mumbled responses from the altar boys. Here the standing, somber people sang in thunderous voices, even though they were singing for a dead man. Hank wondered what kind of heaven Matt Gable had gone to. It probably didn't have nearly naked cherubs blowing trumpets, the way they were painted on the walls of Hank's church.

Afterward the mourners followed the coffin—borne on a hearse pulled by two horses that didn't seem to feel the extra weight—up the hill to the Presbyterian cemetery. Far below, the wide Monongahela River flowed, flanked by smoking mills on both banks. On the river's steel-blue surface, a stern-wheeler pushed coal barges upstream toward the Clairton coke works. Hank watched the barge from the time it appeared around a bend of the river on his left until it drifted beyond his view around a bend to the right.

He'd seen Death. Even though his brother had kept him from staring at it, he'd seen Matt die. The scene tormented Hank so much that in the two days since it happened, it had played itself again and again on the insides of his eyelids like a movie at the nickelodeon, the reels never stopping, but running end to end. The orange, burning heat, the sparks, Matt collapsing into the molten iron without even crying out, the thunder of the falling ladle that echoed still—Hank could bring back that sound whenever he wanted to. Even when he didn't want it. Even standing out there in the open in the quiet cemetery.

Rather than watching the men who strained to lower the heavy coffin into the ground, Hank kept his eyes on the coal barge churning up the river. He could hear the minister praying over the open grave, and then he heard a soft thud. That made him look to see what it was. Matt's widow, heavily veiled in black, had dropped a clump of earth onto the coffin. Quickly Hank looked away again, to the top of the cemetery hill.

Standing there alone, separate from the mourners, was Billy Radichevych. The April breeze fluttered the sleeves of his white shirt. Billy raised his hand in a small wave. When Hank waved back, his father frowned at him. Pay attention to the burial service, the frown meant.

A deep sigh escaped Hank's chest, taking a bit of the terror with it. His best friend was there for him. Billy was there, even though he stood far away on the top of the hill.

Hank wondered if Billy had noticed his new long pants.

4

July 4, 1917

The crowd stood four deep at the edges of the street, not counting
the littlest kids sitting on the curbs. Never had Hank seen
so many American flags in one place. Babies wore them
pinned to their dresses; young women waved them in time
to the music. Members of the Canaan Civic Chorale, all
dressed in white, marched in rectangular formation, holding the edges of an American flag as big as the Kerner
family's kitchen floor. Bigger than their parlor floor. "My
country, 'tis of thee . . ." they sang as they passed.

Hank and Billy wiggled through the mob to hunch down
on the curbstone. Squatting low like that, they didn't ob-
struct the view of anyone behind them.

After the Chorale came the high-school band, led by its
popular drum major—a midget, who skillfully balanced

on his head a tall, white, plumed beaver hat. The band's brass instruments caught the morning sun's rays to gleam like fire, and the satin stripes on the sides of the band members' trousers glowed and rippled as they bent their knees to march in place, keeping time but not playing any music. They waited for the unit behind them to catch up.

A hundred young men in khaki uniforms, a platoon of recruits stationed in Pittsburgh, had been lent to the city of Canaan for the Fourth of July parade. Only a dozen of the soldiers were actually from Canaan; the rest were strangers, but it didn't matter—all of them looked like gods to Hank as they marched forward in straight lines. At the precise moment the first row drew abreast of Hank and Billy, the high-school band struck up "Over There."

The blare of horns electrified Hank, made the hairs on his arms stand straight up. Everyone began to sing, "Over there, over there, send the word, send the word, to beware. For the Yanks are coming. . . ."

Billy and Hank couldn't help themselves: They jumped up, not caring if any little kids behind them couldn't see. They bounced on the balls of their feet and bellowed as loudly as they could make their voices go, "Say a prayer, say a prayer, say a prayer for the boys over there. We will be over, we're coming over, and we won't! be! back! till it's over, over there!"

Frenzied, they joined half a hundred other boys and some girls, too, who fell in line to march behind the platoon of soldiers, and followed them all the way to the parade's end at City Hall, cheering themselves hoarse.

Hank grabbed Billy's arm and yelled, "We gotta get a flag. Where'd all these people get all these flags?" Raised hands everywhere were wildly waving the Stars and Stripes.

"Ask someone," Billy cried. "The flags all look the same, so people must be getting them from the same place. Only I don't want to spend money on one—I want to keep the money I have for the picnic at the park."

A man overheard Billy and said, "You can get 'em free fer nothin' at McToole's Saloon, sonny."

"You mean really free?" Billy asked.

"Yeah, free fer nothin', as long as you pay for a schooner of beer." The man guffawed and slapped his thighs.

"Let's go get some flags," Billy told Hank, and started across the street.

"Wait! Billy, wait!" Hank cried, catching up. "We can't go into a saloon. My mother would kill me! Anyway, the man said you gotta buy beer to get a flag."

Billy paused to consider. "Maybe if some guys in there already bought a lot of beer and got a lot of flags, they'd give us some. It's worth a try."

Hank almost danced with indecision. Billy's words had a certain logic—a man who'd bought five beers would have five flags, and after five beers he'd probably be jolly enough to share a couple of flags with a couple of boys.

Billy was already heading across the street without waiting to see whether Hank followed. Hank hesitated—if his mother found out, she'd have a shouting fit and wouldn't allow him out of the house for the rest of the summer. Still . . . "Wait for me," he yelled, and ran to catch up. Together, they pushed through the swinging doors.

So many mugs of beer and shots of whiskey had been poured in McToole's Saloon that a blind man might have

33

thought the walls were built from beer kegs and whiskey barrels, they smelled so strongly of drink. Even worse than the smell was the din of men shouting in a dozen languages.

"McToole, over here! I need a beer before I croak."

"Whiskey, boss. *Prosze, daj wodki*."

"McToole, you bleedin' Irisher, get the lead out!"

"*Un'uomo potrebbe morire da sete.* Whatsa matta you, McToole?"

The place was packed with steelworkers drinking hard and fast on their day off. Socializing had to take place in one day; the next day off was five months away. Steelworkers got only two paid holidays a year—Christmas and the Fourth of July.

"Where are the flags?" Hank tried to speak quietly to stay inconspicuous, but in the din, Billy couldn't hear him.

Tall enough to see around the heads of the men in the crowd, Billy cried, "I see them. They're in a big jar on top of the bar." He plowed into the crowd and Hank followed, letting Billy push ahead of him. Hank felt swallowed by the press of steelworkers. He fought the urge to grab on to Billy's sleeve.

Laughter burst out from a group of men who were staring at the two boys in their midst. One of them said something in Slovak or Russian or Hungarian; Hank couldn't understand any foreign languages. But Billy blushed.

"What'd he say?" Hank asked.

"He said we look like two pretty girls," Billy muttered.

In a way, Billy did look almost pretty. The roundness of his face nearly hid his prominent Slavic cheekbones. His cheeks were apple red and downy, his lips redder than

34

most girls'. His straight, light-brown hair shone with gold highlights, even in the dimness of McToole's.

Another of the men reached out a hand. Not toward Billy, toward Hank! "Pretty, yes?" he said in English.

Hank jerked backward, but in the jammed room he couldn't squirm out of range. With an open palm, the man patted Hank's cheek several times while the others laughed uproariously and Hank recoiled.

Suddenly the silly, drunken look on the man's face changed to alarm as a big, dirty hand grabbed him by the back of the neck.

A deep voice asked, "Hey, Hank! Someone givin' you trouble, brother-in-law?" Hank didn't need to turn around to know who his savior was. No one else had a voice like Jame Culley's.

"I said, is this here greenhorn givin' you trouble, brother-in-law?" Jame asked again, squeezing the troublemaker's neck until the man's eyes bulged. Then the eyes widened in fear as the man tilted back his head to see all the way up to Jame's face. When Jame let him go, the man tried to squirm his way around Jame's bulk, but Jame stood planted firmly in front of him.

"You wanna fight, John?" Jame asked him softly. "Pickin' on little boys like that, you must be just spoilin' for a fight. But you know what, John?" Jame bent down until his eyes were nearly level with the frightened man's. "I bet you couldn't hit the bartender on the bum with a beer mug, could you, John? *Jak sie mas*."

The noise in the saloon subsided as the other drinkers watched, with interest, to see whether a fight was starting. In a stage whisper, Jame confided to Hank, "I don't know

35

what the hell *jak sie mas* means. It's just something these greenhorns say to each other all the time."

"It means 'how are you,' " Billy mumbled.

"I don't know if this guy's name is John, either," Jame went on in the same loud whisper. "But most greenhorns are John. Or Steve. Or Mike."

While Jame's attention was on the two boys, the man bolted around him and ran out the door. Jame threw back his head and laughed. He swung his head to include in the laughter all the other drinkers, immigrant and American.

He was dirty—clothes, face, hands; his red hair looked tarnished. Only his green eyes and square teeth showed clean through the dirt. Growing stern, he asked, "Now! What are you two kids doing in a place like this?" Since Jame was married to Hank's sister, Kathleen, he had a right, as a relative, to demand to know.

"Some guy outside told us McToole's was giving away American flags for the Fourth of July," Hank answered. "We just wanted a couple, that's all."

"Well, hell, take some, then." Jame picked up the big jar; it looked like the kind that had once held pickled pigs' feet. He thrust it in front of Hank's face and told him, "Take as many flags as you want. McToole won't mind, will you McToole?"

The bartender grinned and said, "If you drink about a dozen boilermakers, Jame, that'll cover the cost."

"Well, that ain't even gonna be hard." Jame pulled a droll face, and half the men standing around the bar laughed loudly along with him. Jame Culley, whose feats of strength and stamina were legendary in Canaan, was a favorite with everyone.

"I been workin' twenty straight hours," he told them, leaning against the counter, bulging his muscles. "For the war effort. So I deserve a few drinks to wash down all the ore dust and cinders I swallowed in the mill. Right?"

"Right! You bet, Jame," the men around him agreed.

Jame downed a shot of whisky and a mug of beer without coming up for breath, then asked, "You kids on your way to Kennywood Park for today's doin's?"

Hank nodded.

"Well, have fun," Jame said. "And Hank, I won't tell your mom about you bein' in here, but don't let it happen again. Hear me?"

Hank nodded. Jame didn't need to make him promise. His skin still felt tainted from the touch of the stranger's callused hand. He swiped at his cheek with his shirtsleeve to rub off the feel of it before he turned to leave.

Billy stayed behind. "Those men . . ." he said, looking up at Jame, "they didn't mean us any harm. They wouldn't have hurt us. They were only teasing."

"I know. I wasn't plannin' to hurt that greenhorn none, either," Jame said. "I was just teasin' 'im back."

The crowd parted to let the two boys through, now that everyone knew they were being watched over by Jame Culley. When Hank pushed open the door, his hands full of American flags, the outside air smelled fresh by comparison, even though it was saturated with mill smells.

Subdued, Billy said to Hank, "My father's a greenhorn, like those guys that bothered us in there. Greenhorn's just a different way of saying Hunkie. That's what I am, too."

"No you're not," Hank told him. "You're an American now." He thrust the half-dozen flags into Billy's hands.

37

5

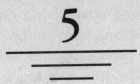

Hank wanted to take the streetcar to Kennywood Park; Billy didn't want to spend the money. Hank had been given money for the park by his parents; Billy had earned his— hoeing the neighbors' gardens; hauling ashes; searching for empty soda-pop bottles and returning them to the grocer, who paid a penny a bottle.

"It's only a mile," Billy argued as the streetcar came into sight. "Anyway, look at it—it's packed."

That was true: Inside the streetcar, people stood jammed together like upright clothespins in a box, rocking forward in unison as the streetcar braked. A few people got on at the stop, but Billy grabbed Hank's arm and propelled him to the other side of the street to keep him from boarding.

By walking fast, they reached Kennywood in fifteen minutes. Hank loved the sounds in the amusement park, sounds that seemed to hover above the tops of the abundant shade trees: wheezy calliope music from the merry-go-round; the roller-coaster crowd's laughter and screams that swelled each time the coaster reached the top of the tracks and thundered downward; a strolling brass band heavy on the tubas. And he loved the smells—sweetness from the beds of petunias planted along the walkways, sourness from spilled ice cream spoiling on the asphalt, the sugary scent of cotton candy, the buttery aroma of popcorn.

"Roller coaster first!" Hank shouted, and started to run, with Billy following. They darted zigzag through hordes of holiday celebrants, not stopping when they nearly toppled small children and once knocked a parasol from the hand of a stout lady.

At each ride the lines were long, but they didn't care. It was ninety-six degrees in the shade, but that didn't bother them, either. Billy wore lightweight cream-colored trousers that were cooler than the ones Hank had on. Hank owned only the one pair of long pants, the heavy blue serge.

On the fast rides, they held up their American flags to make them flap in the wind. On the slow rides they stuck the flags into the buttonholes of their white shirts; both wore three flags in descending order on their shirt-fronts.

They went on every ride twice—at least on everything they considered a good ride. The mild ones, like the merry-go-round and the Ferris wheel, they skipped. Between rides they ate four hot dogs apiece, a cone of cotton candy, and two ice-cream cones. By late afternoon, Billy looked worried as he counted his money.

"If you run out," Hank told him, "we'll find Karl. He'll be here for the dance tonight. He'll give us money if I ask him to."

"I can't take money from Karl," Billy said. "I'll just stretch out what I have left. Hey, look over there."

Hank looked, but couldn't see anything of particular interest. "What?"

"Dorie and Dove Wunderly. From school."

"So?"

After another glance at the coins in his hand, Billy said, "Let's take them on a ride."

"Why?" Hank asked, but Billy was already cutting through the crowd to catch up to the girls.

Dorie and Dove were supposed to be twins, although they didn't look much alike. Dove was petite, blond, dimpled—and silly, Hank thought. Dorie looked about twice as big as Dove, and had started to round out in front like a woman. Since the twins always dressed alike, this caused some odd differences in the way their clothes fit.

When Hank caught up to them, silly little Dove had her hand on Billy's arm and was looking up at him, smiling. "I just love the miniature railroad," she sighed.

That was one of the rides Hank and Billy had avoided all day because it was so dull—nothing but sitting on wooden benches in imitation railroad cars while a small-scale locomotive chugged around part of the park. It was about as exciting as riding the streetcar.

"It's one of my favorites, too," Billy said. Hank stared at him in disbelief.

"We'll get the tickets," Billy told Dove, and yanked Hank by the arm toward the ticket booth. "I'll pay for Dove, and you pay for Dorie," he whispered to Hank.

"Are you crazy?" Hank sputtered. "You're worried about running out of money and you want to waste it on those two?"

"No, I want to *spend* it on Dove. You're going to buy a ticket for Dorie. You sit with Dorie; I'll sit with Dove." Billy had already slid two nickels onto the ticket counter; he pried a dime from Hank's fist and told the ticket woman, "Four for the miniature railroad."

Billy's behavior was so unusual that Hank didn't know how to argue. He found himself waiting in line with Dorie Wunderly, who stood a whole head taller than Hank, even though they were in the same grade. Ahead of them, Billy towered over Dove, which meant that she had to look up to him when he spoke. Dorie didn't bother to look down at Hank, which was fine with him because he didn't intend to talk to her, anyway.

Since the miniature railroad was such a boring ride, not many people waited in the line, so they got through it quickly. Billy took Dove's elbow to help her into her seat, as if she needed any help. Dorie climbed aboard ahead of Hank and plunked herself down. "Billy Radish is cute," she announced when Hank sat beside her, leaving as much space between them as possible. "Why are you wearing long pants?" she asked next. "You're not old enough."

"Neither is Billy."

"But he's a whole lot bigger than you, so long pants look right on him," Dorie announced. After that she had nothing more to say, but turned to look at the scenery, such as it was.

Through the trees, Hank noticed the wide waters of the Monongahela pouring over a lock that had been opened to lower the river level. Since the river flowed past the mill before it reached Kennywood Park, it was already full of strong alkalis, acids, oils, lubricants, granulated slag, and other wastes dumped directly from the steelworks into the river. But people swam in it. As Hank watched, men in bathing trunks jumped off a wooden float into the water, laughing and holding their noses while they sank.

At the end of the ride, Billy handed Dove off the car as carefully as he'd put her into it. Hank got off without looking back—any girl as big and strong as Dorie could get herself off a ride without his help.

"Well," Billy said when they were back on the walkway, "what would you girls like to do now?"

"Huh?" Hank blurted. Both girls giggled.

"You're not a girl, Hank," Dove twittered.

"Are you sure?" Dorie cracked.

Billy's cheeks were redder than usual. Maybe from a day in the sun. More likely, Hank thought, because he'd just invited the Wunderly sisters on what sounded like another ride, and he was nearly out of money. Hank couldn't figure out what was going on inside Billy's head.

"Want a flag?" Billy asked, holding out one of his American flags to Dove. "You give one of yours to Dorie, Hank," he ordered.

"No thanks," Hank said. He didn't care if he sounded rude. After all, it was Hank's brother-in-law who'd gotten the flags for them—if it hadn't been for Jame Culley, they wouldn't have any flags at all. Let Billy give his away if he wanted to. Hank intended to keep all three of his own.

"Don't be so stingy. They were free, weren't they?" Billy said. "We got them in a saloon."

"*He* went into a saloon?" Dorie exclaimed, pointing at Hank, as though she could believe Billy Radish might be bold enough to enter a public tavern, but not Hank Kerner.

"That just made me think of something," Dove said, twisting a blond curl around her finger. "It's so hot, we could maybe cool off if we had something nice and cool to drink. An ice-cream soda would be cooling, wouldn't it, Dorie?"

"Let's get one, then," Billy said. Now he'd started to sweat because he didn't have enough money to buy sodas for himself and Dove. Hank still had enough to buy sodas for all four of them if he wanted to, but he was danged if he would. Billy got himself into this, so let's see him wiggle out of it, he thought.

They began to walk toward the ice-cream pavilion, Billy and Dove ahead, her hand on his sleeve again. Behind them clumped Hank and Dorie, both of them scowling.

"Look, Dove," Dorie called to her twin sister. "Up ahead there. It's Ralph Qualls and Ernie Ingram. Ernie's sweet on Dove," she confided to Hank.

Hank thought if a boy had to be sweet on one of the Wunderly twins, it would probably be Dove, although

Hank didn't like either of them much. At least big Dorie was smart in school. Little Dove was what his mother would call "a pretty twit with more simper than sense."

He recognized the two boys coming toward them. Ralph Qualls and Ernie Ingram were both thirteen, the same age as Billy, but they were a grade ahead of him since Billy had been late starting school in America. The two beefy boys liked to swagger around the school yard and lord it over the smaller kids, including Hank. Right then they were swaggering through the park, too, laughing and shoving each other sideways, taking up more space than they should have.

"Hello, Ralph. Hello, Ernie," Dorie called out.

"Well, look what's comin' up on the menu," Ernie exclaimed when he caught sight of the twins. "Two sweetie pies."

"Yeah, but look what comes with them," Ralph said. "Horseradish and Shrimp."

Ernie laughed uproariously and butted shoulders with Ralph over the joke. Then his mouth twisted into a scowl. "Why are you hanging around my girl, Horseradish?" he demanded, poking Billy on the chest.

"I didn't—uh—know—" Billy stammered. He turned to Dove and asked, "Are you really his girl?"

"Maybe yes, maybe no," she answered. "I'm not telling."

"If I say she is, you don't have to ask her," Ernie growled. "Now get out of my way, Horseradish." He shoved Billy harder.

"Quit pushing me," Billy said quietly.

"Yeah? Who's gonna make me quit? You and Shrimp?"

45

Ernie jerked a thumb toward Hank. "He's too puny to squash a bedbug."

"Yeah, how come you're in long pants, Puny?" Ralph demanded.

"Puny? You mean me? I thought I was Shrimp." Hank tried to turn it into a joke. Better to be laughed at than mauled by those two ogres.

Ralph wouldn't let up. "How old are you, anyway, you puny shrimp?"

"I'm a year behind you in school," Hank stalled. "I'll be in seventh grade. Same as Billy."

"I know how old Hank Kerner is," Dorie Wunderly stated. "I saw it once in the teacher's record book. He skipped a grade, so he's the baby of the class. *Really* a baby!" She waited to make certain everyone was looking at her, then announced it loudly enough for half the park to hear. "Hank Kerner is only ten years old."

"Ten!" Ralph and Ernie exploded into hoots of ridicule. Billy blushed. Dove squealed and covered her mouth. Dorie looked smug.

"Eleven!" Hank howled. "I'm nearly eleven! My birthday's next month! I'll be eleven!" But no one was listening to him. Ralph and Ernie kept hooting and pointing at him, while Billy's face grew even redder.

"Ten years old and he's in long pants!" Ernie yelled. "We gotta do something about that, Qualls."

"Yeah," Ralph Qualls agreed. "It's like he's disguised as a grown-up. Maybe he's really a spy. For the Germans."

"Yeah. His last name's Kerner—that's German. He's a stinkin' Kraut."

"A stinkin' Kraut hangin' around with a dumb Hunkie. No wonder they stick together. No one else wants them." Ralph and Ernie had stopped clowning; they were edging into menace.

"My mother's Irish," Hank tried to tell them, but his thin voice had no power against the already deepened voices of Ralph and Ernie, who could outshout the calliope. Billy said nothing. His glance kept darting from Ralph to Ernie as he tried to estimate the amount of trouble coming up.

Grinning nastily, Ernie leaned an elbow on Ralph's shoulder. "Krauts are mad dogs. You ever hear about that, Qualls? They're worse than mad dogs. I saw it in a newspaper drawing, that those filthy mad-dog German Krauts cut off women's ti— uh, bosoms," Ernie amended, cleaning up his language in deference to the girls. "With bayonets, they cut 'em right off and leave the poor Frog women screamin' and bleedin'. Over in France. Or maybe Belgium. I forget where—it was in the paper."

Dorie and Dove hid their eyes and heaved horrified gasps. Ralph licked his lips.

"Krauts are butchers!" Ernie yelled. "And Kerner here is a German Kraut mad-dog butcher spy! I think we ought to . . . uh . . . how do you say it? *Expose* him to the authorities."

"*Expose* him," Ralph echoed. "I get it. Yeah. Heh-heh. Great idea." The two of them moved toward Hank. "First we'll *expose* what's underneath those long pants."

Ernie's hand shot out toward Hank's belt, but before it made contact, Billy threw himself in front of the two eighth graders. He knocked Ernie onto his butt and grabbed a handful of Ralph's shirtfront as he shouted, "Run, Hank!"

Hank didn't wait for a second invitation—he took off racing. Getting beat up was one thing, but the humiliation of having his pants pulled off in public would have been unbearable. The crowd was so thick that in less than a minute he'd disappeared from the bullies' view, but he kept running for another minute before he slowed down to look back.

Billy was nowhere in sight. Well, Hank was a faster runner than Billy, or maybe Billy had run in a different direction to confuse the two hulks. Hank slipped behind the thick trunk of a shade maple to wait. Hidden like that, he could keep an eye out for Billy.

More minutes passed, and Hank began to do some serious worrying. What if Billy hadn't run? What if he couldn't? Ralph and Ernie might have held on to him, or knocked him down. If Billy couldn't escape, they'd whale the living tar out of him! Maybe hurt him bad.

He left the concealment of the tree and scanned the crowds. "Could you tell me the time, mister?" he asked a passing man.

"Sure, kid." The man dug out his pocket watch and said, "Eighteen minutes past six."

Kennywood Park covered forty-some acres filled with pavilions, rides, food stands, penny arcades, flower beds, shade trees, and on this most important day of the summer, thousands of people of all sizes, shapes, and ages. Finding someone in that mob would be hard. Hank went back to the miniature railroad, but there was no trace of Billy,

Ralph, Ernie, or the Wunderly twins, so he circled the area around the ride, fanning out into larger and larger circles. By a quarter past seven he still hadn't found Billy.

In desperation, Hank bought a ticket for the Ferris wheel. Maybe if he got high enough, he could see Billy and could yell to get his attention.

The shadows had lengthened; lighted globes on the Ferris wheel revolved symmetrically. Hank was one of the last to get on before a chain blocked off the next batch of riders. The only space left was in a car with a woman and a little boy about six years old, who clung to his mother and whimpered.

"Don't be afraid," the woman told her child. "The ride isn't frightening at all. See this little boy next to you?" She pointed at Hank. "He isn't afraid, and he's not much older than you."

Hank gave the kid a ferocious look. He'd have gotten off right then if the attendant hadn't already snapped the bar in place, locking the three of them into an interminable circling on the big, lighted wheel. He had a wicked desire to rock the car back and forth hard, to really scare the little kid witless, but the mother was sitting right there.

From high in the air, he saw a dozen different boys who could have been Billy. Looking down on the tops of their heads, it was impossible to tell for sure. No point yelling; the brass band blared right next to the Ferris wheel, drowning out people's shouts.

He was surprised to notice the number of khaki uniforms sprinkled through the crowd. An awful lot of soldiers must have been given leave for the holiday, maybe their last leaves before being shipped to France. He began to look for white sailor hats, too, but there were only a handful. Then he reminded himself that he was supposed to be searching for Billy.

It was hopeless. It had been a stupid idea to get stuck on that Ferris wheel. He hung out of the car and banged the side with his palm, wondering if the man who ran the ride had died or something, and couldn't bring the torturous winding to a halt. Down, up, down, up. At last the attendant began to stop the cars, one by one, to let people off. When the wheel jerked to a stop with Hank's car at the very top, rocking from the sudden braking, the kid next to him really went hysterical. Naturally, theirs was the last car to be emptied. When it reached the bottom, Hank didn't wait for the bar to be unlatched—he wiggled out from underneath it and leaped over the side of the car.

On the walkway once more, he headed toward the dance pavilion. Karl was supposed to go there with Margie for the dancing that would begin at eight. It was only a quarter to eight, but Hank would wait and ask Karl for help in finding Billy. Ralph and Ernie might have beat Billy to a bloody pulp and dumped him someplace—a knot of fear caught in Hank's throat at the possibility. Karl would know whether or not to call the park police.

"Hi," Billy said, appearing from nowhere.

"Where the heck have you been!" Hank yelled.

"In the men's room. Trying to get cleaned up. Then I was all over the park looking for you, but I couldn't find you."

"Me, too. I couldn't find you, either. I was worried sick."

Billy's cream-colored pants showed black asphalt smears. His American flags were gone because the front of his shirt had been ripped buttonless. Hank instinctively looked down, and saw that all three of his own flags were still in place, stuck in his buttonholes. They looked pretty childish.

"What'd they do to you?" Hank demanded. "Are you hurt bad?"

"Not too bad." The skin over Billy's left cheekbone was split; the flesh looked puffy and purple. Blood stained his shirt, but he'd cleaned his face, probably with the wet handkerchief wrapped around his knuckles.

"Did they break anything? Is your hand all right?"

"No. Yes. They didn't break anything. My hand's just skinned. Dorie and Dove went off with them." Billy shook his head. "If you were only bigger," he said, eyeing Hank accusingly, "we could have beat up those guys, and the girls would have gone with us."

"Are you nuts?" Hank was so astounded he could hardly speak. "You mean . . . you'd have fought over those dumb girls? Over *Dorie and Dove Wunderly?*"

"Grow up, Hank," Billy said, and turned abruptly toward the dance pavilion, where the musicians were beginning to tune up. Shoulders hunched, he leaned against a post and watched the dance floor.

Hank stared at Billy, trying to decipher the strange expression on his face. "Are you hungry?" he asked uncertainly. Maybe that was the problem. Billy was a big boy, and he always needed a lot to eat. "We could buy something."

"With what? All my money's gone," Billy said, indignant. "They took it. They said I wouldn't know the difference, because Hunkies are so dumb they can't count, anyway."

"Yeah, and they called me a stinkin' Kraut!" Hank cried. "Where do those bums get off, calling me names like that?"

Billy turned around. His lips might just have been swollen from a hard punch, or they might have been twisted in a wry smile. He said nothing.

"There's Karl and Margie," Hank noticed, pointing to the dance floor.

The musicians were still tuning up. Holding hands, Karl and Margie stood against the far wall, waiting with a hundred other young couples, the men clean-shaven and well pressed, the girls in soft summer dresses that clung to their warm, damp bodies.

Margie was Mary Margaret Culley, sister of Jame Culley, who was married to Kathleen, who was Karl and Hank's sister. When Karl and Margie got married the following month, a Kerner brother and sister would have married a Culley sister and brother. If Karl and Margie had children, they would be double cousins to Jame and Kathleen's two little boys. Hank thought that was pretty interesting. He'd never heard of any other families in Canaan where a brother and sister had married another brother and sister.

"I'll go get some money from Karl," he said, but before he could start across the floor, the orchestra began to play "Poor Butterfly."

The opening chords of the music set off the scraping of hundreds of shoe soles as couples shuffled onto the dance floor. Hank lost sight of Karl and Margie for a moment. When he found them again, they were already dancing.

For a girl, Margie was tall; Karl stood six feet two and Margie's forehead rested against his chin. Her hair was red-gold, the same color as her brother Jame's. She wore a loose, filmy, pale green dress with a scalloped hem that stopped several inches above her ankles. If Hank had ever thought about it, he'd have had to admit that she was pretty. As she danced, her movements matched Karl's like a re-flection in a mirror.

"How does it happen like that?" Billy asked.

"What?"

"The way they move together. How does each one know what the other one's going to do?" Billy shifted against the post. "When Ukrainian people dance, they know the steps to the different dances 'cause they learn them at weddings when they're little, but they don't dance holding on to each other like that."

"I don't know," Hank answered, not much interested.

"I'd like to learn to dance like that," Billy said. "You have a Victrola in your house. Maybe we could practice together."

"You and me dance? No thanks!" Hank took a step backward from Billy and squinted at him. "Let's get some-thing to eat," he said. "I have enough money to buy a couple more hot dogs."

"I don't . . ." Billy began.

"Dang it, Billy, the least I can do is buy you a hot dog. You probably saved my life back there. Those guys would have beat the pants off me!" When he realized what he'd said, Hank started to laugh so hard he gasped. "Did you hear that? The pants off me! That's just what they wanted." Mimicking a girl's high, quavery voice, Hank cried, "Oh Bazyli, you hero, you saved my southern pride. I mean my very southernest pride, right here." He twisted to poke out his skinny butt.

Laughing, Billy took a swipe at him.

"Come on," Hank said. "Let's go eat. I still have enough for hot dogs and root beer."

"Yeah. And then it'll be time for fireworks."

Hank stopped. All day long he'd been figuring out ways to leave the park before the fireworks started. He'd planned to invite Billy to a movie back in town—Hank's treat. A Tom Mix film was playing at the Orpheum. They could have left the park sooner, if they hadn't become separated after the fight with Ralph and Ernie.

"You really want to watch the fireworks?" he asked Billy.

"Sure I want to see them," Billy answered. "That's the best part of the whole Fourth of July."

Hank closed his eyes, dreading what lay ahead. He knew the brilliant flares and sparks in the sky would bring back images of molten iron spilling all over the open hearth. He would try to keep his eyes closed when rockets exploded like angry golden bees, right above his head. And if he cried, thinking of Matt Gable, no one would notice in the dark.

After all, he owed it to Billy to stay, since that was what

Billy wanted. Hank needed to make amends for behaving like a coward, for running away, leaving his friend to do battle alone. Remembering it, he was ashamed.

"Come on, Billy, I'll buy you *three* hot dogs," he said.

6

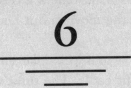

August 18, 1917

Karl Kerner married Margie Culley at 9:30 on Saturday morn-ing, at the altar of Holy Name Church. Because Saturday was a work day, only family members and a few neighbors attended the wedding. Karl, his father Hugo, and his best man Jame Culley had all taken the day off without pay.

Before the ceremony, Jame led the few guests one by one to their proper places. In the right front pew sat the Kerners: Hugo, Maggie Rose, and Hank; to the left were the Culleys: Margie's parents Mayo and Bridey, her sisters Mary Eileen, Mary Agnes, and Mary Frances. And in the middle of the Culleys sat their second son, Francis X, slouching a little, smiling slightly.

Hank tried to keep his eyes straight ahead on the altar. Margie was as pretty as a bridal advertisement in her white dress and wide-brimmed lace hat. Hank's sister Kathleen, who was matron of honor, wore a pale yellow dress—a striking contrast to her dark, wavy hair. Karl's suit had been hand-tailored by Mr. Levine, and for once Jame looked as neat as Karl. Altogether, the four young people at the altar made as handsome a group as any Hank had ever seen, even in the movies. But his gaze kept straying to Francis X Culley.

Francis X wore a uniform! Like all government-issue army uniforms, it fit badly. The tunic's high "dog collar" circled the young soldier's neck with too many inches to spare; the sleeves were so long that the cuffs touched his knuckles; the military riding breeches, snug at the knee and baggy in the seat, drooped; and the puttees—long strips of wool wrapped around his legs from knees to ankles—were crooked. Nevertheless, Francis X was in the khaki uniform of an American Expeditionary Forces soldier, and Hank thought he looked splendid.

After the wedding everyone else clustered around the bride and groom, but Hank headed for Francis X.

"Want to try on my cap?" Francis X asked him.

"Sure! Thanks!" Reverently, Hank put on the army overseas cap. What would it be like to be a soldier on the way to France? "Will you ship out pretty soon?" he asked.

"My leave's up in a week, then I head for Camp Pendleton. That's in New Jersey. That's where they'll load us onto the big ocean liner to sail overseas." Francis X spoke carelessly, as if all the coming excitement were just part of a day's work. He pulled a cigarette from his tunic pocket and a wooden match from his pants pocket.

"Watch this," he told Hank, as he swiped the match head

against the wool of his breeches. The flame flared up and he lit the cigarette. "See, this military cloth is so tough you can light a match on it. Too bad it ain't tough enough to stop bullets." He grinned, and stuck the cigarette into the corner of his mouth.

Such bravery awed Hank—imagine joking about being hit by a bullet! "I bet you're pretty good at shooting a gun, huh, Francis X?" he asked.

"You bet. Enfield .30.06 rifle. I was top marksman in my unit. Not just with the Enfield—I got the best score with the Browning .30 caliber machine gun, too. What a gun—*a-a-a-a-a*!" Francis X crouched over an imaginary Browning. "One of them babies spits out six hundred rounds a minute, Hank. Can't wait till I get over there and start poppin' off some Huns. Bang bang bang. *A-a-a-a-a*!"

When Francis X faked the machine-gun sounds, he seemed like a little kid. For a seventeen-year-old, Francis X Culley was definitely undersized—no wonder the uniform didn't fit him right. His brother Jame was a giant by comparison, but then their mother, Bridey Culley, stood less than five feet tall. And the father, Mayo Culley, was thin as a broomstick.

Francis X flipped the cigarette down the church steps, then took out a wrinkled handkerchief and began to polish the brass buttons on the collar of his tunic, although they already gleamed. Watching him, wishing he had buttons like that, Hank turned just in time to see Karl and Margie run down the church steps.

"Throw some rice!" Hank's mother told him, thrusting out a paper bag. "Grab a handful. It's for good luck."

"They'll need some luck so Karl don't get drafted," Francis X said. "Me—I didn't wait for the draft. I enlisted." It sounded just a shade cocky, but then, maybe Francis X had a right to be cocky. After all, he was going to France. "Hey, Hank," he said, "better give back my cap before you forget to—accidentally on purpose, right? Ha-ha."

The wedding reception began at four that afternoon at the mansion of Charles Bonner, general superintendent of the Canaan Works of the Carnegie Steel Company. For five years Margie had been employed as a maid in the Bonner household. During that time, under the guidance of Bonner's wife, Yulyona, Margie had blossomed from a shy, almost speechless girl to the confident, attractive bride cutting cake at the reception.

"This is a special day for Charles and me," Yulyona Bonner announced to the more than a hundred guests crowded into the Bonner library. "Margie has become like a daughter to us—well, let me amend that to sister. I don't think I'm quite old enough to qualify as her mother."

"I'm plenty old enough to qualify as her father," Charles Bonner quipped, his long, aristocratic face wreathed in smiles. The guests' laughter was a bit restrained. Since most of them labored in the mill where Charles Bonner was as powerful as God, they weren't sure how to react when he joked about himself. Laugh to show they got the joke? Or shake their heads to let him know they didn't consider him especially old?

Yulyona continued, "If Margie is important to us, so is Karl. He was my pupil the first year I taught at Canaan

High School. First and only year," she added ruefully, "since I lost my teaching job when I got married." Raising a wine glass in salute, she declared, "We wish the very best to this wonderful young couple. May this be a day they will always remember with gladness. Please, everyone, enjoy yourselves."

"Well, let's enjoy ourselves, then," Hank told Billy. "Look at all those fancy cakes. And that big fish—Karl said it's a salmon and it got shipped all the way from the state of Washington. By train, packed in ice."

When Hank had asked if he could bring Billy to the reception, his mother had said, "It's fine with me. He'll keep you company so you won't get bored with all the grown-up doings. But behave yourselves. Remember who the Bonners are. Your father and your brother work in the mill, and so will you before long. I wouldn't want you to disgrace the Kerner family by running or yelling or misbehaving in front of Superintendent Bonner."

Most of the dozens of mill workers who came as guests had never seen the inside of the mansion. Their wives walked around the edges of the large room, examining, but never touching, the furniture, its upholstery, the carpets, the drapes, the golden cords on the drapery pulls, the lamps on the tables, the shades on the lamps, the pictures on the walls, and, with the greatest curiosity of all, they examined Yulyona Petrov Bonner, the immigrant woman who'd become the general superintendent's wife.

Although the room was the coolest in Canaan, because its French doors and eight large windows stood open to catch every breeze, it still felt hot, yet not a man in the

61

room removed his suit coat, or a woman her hat.

"I'm sweating," Hank complained. "I wish I could get all packed up in ice like that fish."

Billy wore a cream-colored jacket that matched his trousers. His suit looked just right for an August afternoon. In his heavy, blue serge suit, Hank was dying from the heat. He helped himself to more lemonade.

A small bite of the salmon convinced him he didn't much like fish that came all the way from Washington State. The cakes were delicious, though. Hank stuffed his mouth with one of them and picked up another one for Billy when he heard someone call out, "Bazyli Radichevych!"

He whirled around to see who had spoken Billy's real name, and was amazed to find Yulyona Bonner, the wife of the general superintendent, shaking Billy's hand. "I'm so pleased that you came, Bazyli," she told him. "Are your parents here?"

"No, I came with Hank. He's Karl's brother. Hank was my first friend when I came to America."

"I'm his best friend," Hank added.

She focused on Hank and said, "You don't look at all like Karl. But then, he was much older when I first met him. Fifteen."

"Just four years older. I'm eleven." He could say it with authority now, since he'd had his birthday.

"Really?" Turning back to Billy, she told him, "Bazyli, please give my warmest regards to your parents. And your sister Zosia—what a beautiful young woman she's becoming."

After she'd moved on to chat with the other guests,

Hank asked, "How does Mrs. Bonner know you?"

"From church. Her father is the cantor at the Russian Orthodox church where we go. She goes there, too. But Mr. Bonner doesn't. He goes to some American church."

Suddenly the polite, subdued murmuring in the crowded room came to a halt. Everyone turned to stare at Francis X Culley, who was shouting, "Size don't matter, dammit! A bullet don't care if you're short or tall. It'll cut down a man if he's six feet four and two hundred thirty pounds . . . and spill his guts all over the place."

"Sure, Fran, sure," Jame said, trying to calm his brother. "Just keep it quiet, okay, buddy?"

Francis X hadn't strayed far from the beer kegs since he'd arrived at the reception. His words slurred as he yelled, "Get your s-stinkin' hands off me, Jame! You might be the biggest Culley, but I'm the one in uniform."

All the guests watched intently, with embarrassment and a touch of anticipation, to see whether the Culley brothers would actually hit each other right there in the superintendent's mansion.

"You're right, Fran," Jame said soothingly. "Size don't count for nothin'. You're as good a man as anyone."

"Damn right!" Francis X swung his arm and knocked a beer glass to the floor; people gasped as the beer spilled all over the Bonners' expensive carpet. Two serving girls hired for the day rushed to clean it up.

"You'll never get into the war, Jame," Francis X cried. "You'll never get over there 'cause you got those two kids. But me—I'll see Paris. I'll see France. I'll see a whole bunch of mademoiselles' underpants, too." At the guests' aghast murmurs, he broke into a loud whinny of laughter.

Short, feisty Bridey Culley stomped up to her sons and clamped a hand on Francis X's arm. "Now you just stop the way you're behavin', Frannie. Stop it this instant!" she demanded. "You're disgracin' the family! Jame, help me get him out of here. He needs fresh air."

They made a mismatched trio: Francis X in the middle, his ankles wobbling, little Bridey reaching up to prop him on the one side, enormous Jame reaching down to hold him up on the other side. Stumbling, they wove through the French doors onto the veranda.

Before any of the assembled guests could breathe a sigh of relief or a whisper of gossip, Kathleen Kerner Culley jumped up. "What this party needs is a little music," she declared, and in a whirl of yellow tulle, seated herself on the piano bench. "You all ought to know this one." She began to play "Smiles."

The next instant Yulyona Bonner reached the piano. With one hand on Kathleen's shoulder she waved the still-flustered guests toward her and cried, "Everyone join in! Come on, sing! *'There are smiles, that make us happy . . .'*"

It wasn't long until almost all of the hundred-or-more guests were singing—after all, as Maggie Rose said later, "When the general superintendent's wife tells you to sing, you sing." But the damage had been done, as far as Hank was concerned. With two marriages now sealing the bond between the Kerners and the Culleys, Francis X Culley was definitely Hank's kin.

Red-faced, Hank muttered to Billy, "Francis X acted like a sap. I hate what he did."

"Don't take it so personal," Billy told him, reaching for another cake on the buffet table. "Anyway, it's no big thing. Every good Ukrainian wedding has at least one fight."

"Honest?" Billy was probably just saying that to make Hank feel better.

Billy nodded. "It's the truth. Without a brawl, the guests feel cheated. Look around this room—no one's stiff anymore. They're starting to have fun."

The crowd did seem to have loosened up. Karl now sat beside Kathleen on the piano bench, hitting the bass keys while she played the higher octaves. It was startling how much they looked alike—no one could miss knowing they were brother and sister. Both had dark hair and very blue eyes, and when they played the piano together, the animation in each one's face was mirrored in the other's. It was Hank who was different: With his small size and straight blond hair, no one would ever take him for their brother. He wasn't even musical.

Margie leaned against the piano, her wide white hat slightly off center, looking adoringly at her new husband. At a pause in the music, she begged, "Play 'Poor Butterfly.' It's my favorite."

Karl and Kathleen riffled into the melody, Karl's broad fingers striking the chords with a thumping rhythm as everyone sang, *"Poor Butterfly, 'neath the blossoms waiting, Poor Butterfly . . ."*

Hank sensed that Billy had moved away from him. When he turned to see where his friend had gone, he noticed him standing in front of Yulyona Bonner, and then . . . Billy bowed!

It was a perfect bow—as polished as if he bowed before a lady every day of his life. "Would you dance with me, Mrs. Bonner?" he asked.

"I'd be honored, Bazyli." She held out her arms to him.

It took a moment for Hank to realize that his mouth was hanging open. He clamped it shut.

Somehow, since the Fourth of July, Billy had learned to dance. He moved a bit stiffly, but his feet knew where they were going, all right. The top of his head was only an inch below Yulyona Bonner's smooth coiffure. As they brushed past Hank, he heard her say, "You're only thirteen, Bazyli? You seem older."

Billy didn't blush or grin; he nodded slightly, as though he were used to women's flattery. When Margie noticed Billy dancing with Yulyona Bonner, she bent and whispered something to Karl, who kept playing chorus after chorus of "Poor Butterfly" to let the two of them dance as long as possible. The wedding guests moved back to give them more room, smiling at the charming picture they made: the tall, nice-looking Ukrainian boy and the beautifully dressed superintendent's wife. Almost all of the guests knew the words; they sang along, *"But if he don't come back, Then I never sigh or cry, I just must die, Poor Butterfly."*

After the dance, after everyone applauded, Billy sidled up to Hank's accusing stare and mumbled, "My sister Zosia taught me. She's been going out with an American boy." When Hank said nothing, Billy added, "So what's wrong with learning to dance? You didn't want to, remember? So I didn't bother you anymore about it."

Before Hank could say that dancing was sissy, he heard

another disturbance in the room, and his heart sank. Francis X again? But it was only a flurry of good wishes because the bride and groom were leaving.

Once more, people threw rice—but only after everyone had rushed outside, because no one wanted to spoil the Bonners' carpet a second time, not even with a single spilled grain of rice. Not after the beer Francis X had dumped.

As the bride and groom drove away in a borrowed automobile—one of several the Bonners owned—Hank told Billy, "I've had enough to eat, and I want to take off this hot suit. So let's get out of here."

"Already? The party's still going on. What's the matter, aren't you having a good time?"

Hank wasn't sure. At first he'd been proud because the rich, important Bonners were so fond of his new sister-in-law that they'd given her a big wedding party. Then Francis X, whom he'd idolized in the morning, had behaved like a loudmouthed boor and embarrassed him. Next he'd felt proud of Karl and Kathleen, his brother and sister, for covering Francis X's crudeness by entertaining at the piano. Everyone seemed to admire them.

And after that, Billy had danced with Yulyona Bonner. And then everyone admired *them*.

"I'm having a really great time," Billy was saying. "It's the best—"

"Let's race! I can beat you running up the hill," Hank interrupted, and tore off along the driveway. Billy would never catch up. Hank had always been able to stay ahead of Billy.

7

January 14, 1918

The clouds hung down like stuffing in a mattress—a dirty, torn mattress. Pine Alley ran narrowly between the back-yards of houses that fronted Chestnut Street on one side and High Street on the other. On the way to Billy's, Hank walked past woodsheds, privies, chicken coops, and piles of trash. He kicked a flattened can; it bounced and slid along the frozen ground.

Even the blue serge suit, a wool overcoat, stocking cap, and scarf couldn't keep the winter cold from penetrating his insides. And he wouldn't have worn all that if his mother hadn't insisted.

"I'm only going up the hill to Billy's," he'd argued.

"It's frigid out and I don't want you getting sick," she'd argued back. "Here—I wrapped his gift in tissue paper. I hope Billy's family will appreciate that these handkerchiefs are pure Irish linen."

"What's it matter whether his family appreciates it or not? It's Billy's present, isn't it?"

"Yes, but fourteen-year-old boys don't know anything about quality, the kind you find in pure Irish linen."

Fourteen. Billy was fourteen today. Now no one could dispute his right to wear long pants. "How come your family's having this big celebration for your birthday this year?" Hank had asked the day before, when they walked home from school together for the last time. "You never had a birthday party any other year."

"It's not really a birthday party," Billy had explained. "It's a name-day celebration. Ukrainian people celebrate the holy day of the saint they were named for. It just happened that I was born on Saint Basil's Day, and they decided to name me Bazyli, so my birthday and my name day are the same day. Most people's aren't."

"Heck, when I thought up a name for you the first day I knew you, maybe it should have been Basil Radish instead of Billy Radish."

"I liked Billy better. It sounded more American."

"You still didn't tell me why you're getting a big party this year," Hank had persisted.

" 'Cause tomorrow I'm fourteen—a man!" When Hank had hooted, Billy had punched him, and they'd wrestled in the snow, each of them trying to shove snow down the other's coat collar.

"Anyone else coming from school?" Hank had asked after they called a truce to the fight and he'd dug his books

70

out of a snowbank.

"No. Just family friends and you. I'm through with school now. I stuck it out till fourteen—that's long enough."

Now Hank trudged up the hill holding the tissue-wrapped gift. Today would be Billy's last and only day of freedom, a day with no school and no work. The following day Billy would start in the steel mill full-time, which meant working twelve hours a day, seven days a week, with a week of day turn followed by a week of night turn, probably for the rest of his life. Yet the prospect didn't seem to bother him a bit.

"I'll be making good wages," he'd said proudly. "At least as long as the war lasts. My father thinks there'll be layoffs after that, but if I'm a good enough worker, maybe they'll keep me on."

The Radichevych house had no front porch, just two sagging steps that led to the door. Before he knocked, Hank could hear voices inside—male voices, deep and jovial. Zosia Radichevych, Billy's sister, opened the door for him.

"Come on in, Hank," she said, sounding altogether American against the background of Old-World voices. Hank remembered Mrs. Bonner saying how beautiful Zosia was becoming. Hank rarely noticed girls' looks, and Zosia at seventeen was more of a woman than a girl, but he had to admit she looked pretty good. In the steamy interior of the small house, where coal smoke, pipe-tobacco smoke, and cooking odors combined with the smell of wet wool coats, Zosia glowed. Damp tendrils of dark hair curled around her flushed cheeks, and her moist lips were redder than Billy's. "Give me your coat, Hank. Bazyli, Hank's here," she announced.

As if she needed to call attention to his arrival! The parlor was so small that the guests had to squeeze together to let Zosia get past with the coat. Tables had been placed side by side; they reached all the way across the room from one wall to the other. Only men stood talking in the parlor; the women were all cooking together in the kitchen, which was even smaller than the parlor.

"Happy name day, *Basil*," Hank told him quietly, aware that most of the men in the room were eyeing Hank, who stood out because he was the youngest and the only non-European. "Here's a present for you. I wanted to get you this swell book I found—*Silent Pete and the Stowaways*—but my mom got this instead."

"Thanks. Let me introduce you." Billy waited for a lull in the talk, then said, first in English and then in Ukrainian, "This is my friend Hank Kerner." Although there was little space to move around in, he went from one man to another, towing Hank and presenting him in the Ukrainian language. The men all responded in Ukrainian, too, so Hank didn't know what they were saying.

"How do you do," he kept repeating, hoping that was right, and that they weren't asking him questions about where he lived or who his father was or anything.

Then the talk changed pitch, and everyone stood a little straighter. Billy told Hank, "The priest is coming up the path. My father just saw him through the window, so I need to leave you for a minute." Mr. Radichevych had beckoned Billy to the door, where, with lighted candles in their hands, both of them stood to greet the arriving dignitary.

The priest's tall black hat—like a top hat without a brim—scraped against the door frame as he entered. All his clothes were black: the heavy overcoat, the suit, the shirtfront, the high boots; and his beard was thick and as black as his clothes. A large gold cross hanging from a chain around his neck stood out amid all the blackness, catching the little light in the room.

Mr. Radichevych bowed before the priest; Billy bowed and kissed his hand while the priest made the sign of the cross—backward from the way they did it in Hank's church—above Billy's head.

The room was so crowded the priest could step forward only a foot or two to accept the greetings of the other men. All of them bowed, some of them three times in a row. Then the priest turned his dark eyes on Hank, who tried to imitate the others by bowing properly, although he felt as stiff as a plank, as though he might splinter by bending himself in half that way. He guessed he must have done it all right, since no one laughed.

Only the men—and that included Hank—would be eating: twelve of them, with the priest in the center, Billy's father on one side of him, Billy on the other. "You can sit next to me," Billy said, and Hank's chest flooded with relief. He seemed to be the only person in the room who spoke only English. If he'd been anywhere but next to Billy, he couldn't have understood a word.

"Where will the women eat?" he asked Billy.

"Oh, they'll have their own party after we get through. Don't worry about them—they like it better that way."

All the men sat on the same side of the table, facing the door, with the kitchen behind them, where the women worked as quietly as possible so they wouldn't interfere with the men's talk. Before the meal began, Zosia brought in a thick-crusted, round loaf of bread and placed it on the table in front of the priest.

The guests bowed their heads. Hank did, too, but he watched out of the corners of his eyes to see what was happening.

The priest stood. His dark hair was parted exactly in the middle and hung down far beneath his collar, where it mingled with the edges of his full beard. The gold crucifix that hung from his neck had three crossbars, rather than just one. As he prayed in Russian, he cut the top crust of the round loaf in the shape of a cross. After pulling the loaf apart at the cuts, he poured red wine into the white bread. By name the priest blessed the members of the Radichevych household: Bogdan, Billy's father; Galya, his mother; Zosia, his sister. Then, with his hand on Billy's head, the priest prayed for somebody named Vasily. It took a moment for Hank to realize that *Vasily* was the Russian way to say *Bazyli*.

"I'm glad that part's over," Billy whispered to Hank. "I'm starved!"

The meal began with beet soup, served from behind by the women. "Do you like the soup?" Billy asked Hank.

"Sure. It's fine. If anyone talks to me—like, asks me a question or anything—you gotta tell me what they say, okay, Billy? I mean, it was nice of you to invite me here, but I feel like a dumbbell. I don't know what's going on, and I can't understand a word!"

"Well, right now the priest is talking about how awful it was that the Bolsheviks killed the czar's family last summer. And about how he's scared the churches will all be closed down by the Red revolutionaries, and that millions of people are freezing and starving to death in Russia this winter."

"Gee, that's too bad," Hank said. "That must make your father feel terrible, to hear sad news like that when people came to your party to have a good time."

"My father? Heck no. He doesn't feel bad. My father is Ukrainian. The more the Russians kill one another, the better he likes it. He hates Russia."

"Huh? But you belong to the Russian church."

Billy shrugged. "Only because there's no Ukrainian Orthodox church in America. It's complicated. Ukrainians hate Russia, but they don't hate the church. The church is God. Nobody can hate God."

From behind, the women kept offering food, arms continually reaching around the men to fill their plates. Hank ate as much as he could, but still the food kept coming: stuffed cabbage; rolled-up chicken breasts; potatoes with parsley; pork; cheese; bread; cucumbers; onions in cream; onions in vinegar; pickles; beets; pickled beets; until every inch of the table held a dish of something or other.

At last the women seemed convinced they couldn't urge another bite on anyone, and they began to clear the plates and bring in pastries. Soon after, the priest left. Instantly the mood in the crowded room turned more boisterous. Even the chatter from the kitchen grew merrier.

Bottles and glasses appeared on the table, one of them in front of Hank.

"What's in this?" he asked Billy.

"Vodka. They're going to drink toasts. You can just hold the glass up to your lips. Don't drink any of it—it's pretty strong stuff."

"Are you going to?"

Billy grinned. "Maybe just a little taste. It's my name day. Starting tomorrow I'm a working man."

Legally, boys couldn't get a job in the steel mills until they'd turned fourteen. Before the war, they were restricted to the easier, safer "boy jobs" until the age of sixteen. With the war came a shortage of mill workers, and bosses looked the other way when fourteen-year-olds filled some of the "man jobs." Billy would start right in on one of the more dangerous "man jobs," as an oiler in the blower room.

As toasts were offered one after another, Billy translated for Hank. "This one's to the Ukraine, the motherland." And next, "To America, the land of freedom." Billy laughed when he explained, "Now they're drinking to Ukrainian women. They said they're beautiful as angels, sweet as ripe peaches, and strong as horses." And a little later, "This one's to me, in honor of my name day."

Hank thought he should taste just a drop of the vodka for that toast. He barely dipped the tip of his tongue into the glass. The liquor burned, but not unpleasantly, tasting a little better than the paregoric his mother gave him when he had a bellyache.

Mr. Radichevych stood up, somewhat unsteadily, and raised his glass. His other hand squeezed Billy's shoulder while he made a rather long speech, then urged Billy, "Tell him. Tell him what I say."

"It's a toast to you, Hank. To you and me." Rising to his feet, Billy translated, "My father said that in America, people from different villages can be like brothers. He said you and I played side by side as children, and we will work side by side as men. And while life lasts, we will stay friends."

All the men smiled at Hank and spoke in tones that showed they agreed with Billy's father. Not sure whether he was supposed to stand up or not, Hank decided he'd better, and realized when he did how much shorter he was than anyone else at the table. Yet they considered him special, he could tell that. He was a real American, the only one in the room born in America. And his father before him had been born in America. Hank was pretty sure they'd all been told that his father was a foreman in the mill—not a common laborer, like they were, but a boss— which elevated him even further. With all that to recommend him, it really was pretty nice for Hank to be best friends with an immigrant boy. He smiled back at the men.

When they raised their glasses, he did, too. When they drank, so did Hank.

And instantly exploded into a choking fit. The vodka set his mouth and throat on fire. He coughed and gasped for air as Billy pounded his back and the men laughed themselves hoarse. Humiliated, Hank collapsed into his chair. Zosia brought him a glass of water, which he couldn't even sip because he was still choking.

His eyes filled with tears, not just from embarrassment but because the vodka burned every cavity in his skull. Billy and his father both leaned over Hank, concerned, and as he looked up at them through brimming eyes, a strange thing happened.

He could see each of Billy's features with perfect clarity: the apple cheeks with downy fuzz above the jaw; the full, reddish lips; gold highlights in the thick brown hair; his straight eyebrows; his long lashes. His youth. Strength. Health. That he was almost grown to full height.

Just behind Billy stood Mr. Radichevych, about thirty years older. The layer of hair on top of his head was thin. Once it had been the color of Billy's, but now white hairs mixed with the brown. His face looked burned from the sun, but since it was midwinter, the ruddiness came from everyday exposure to thousand-degree heat in the mill. Some of his pores were blackened from mill dirt.

It struck Hank how much Billy looked like his father. He'd never noticed it before. But Billy was young and fresh, the sapling of a fruit tree, while Mr. Radichevych looked thickened, coarsened, bowed in the shoulders and curved in the spine, heavy-knuckled, with fingernails thick as bark.

As Hank swung his head from one to the other, he knew that Billy would one day come to look like his father. That's what hard labor in the steel mill would do to him.

But not me, he thought. No matter what anyone says, I won't work in that mill. They can't make me. I won't be like these men.

"I'm all right," he told Billy and his father. "I'll be just fine now."

They believed him, and went on to toast other things.

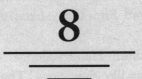

8

July 4, 1918

"You can't wear those pants today," Maggie Rose Kerner told her son.

"I gotta wear 'em!" Hank cried. "This is Billy's citizenship day. It's the most important day of his life. You want me to go to Billy's big day in *knickers?*"

"You'd be better off to go in knickers than in those pants. They're too short for you. I let the cuffs down as far as I could, but they're still too short. You look silly. I can see your shins, almost."

Hank looked down. An inch of stocking showed above the tops of his high-buttoned shoes.

"Then I'll pull them lower at the waist," he said. "Here, loosen my suspenders in the back so I can pull the pants down."

"Hmpf! With your skinny hips, they'll fall right off if you pull them much lower."

"They won't fall down. The suspenders will keep them from falling down."

"You are the most difficult child!" she exclaimed. "Hold still!" From behind him she yanked on the suspenders, adjusting them.

"Mom, I'll be late!" Hank yelled.

"Don't pull away like that, or—" The warning came too late—the suspenders snapped against his back with a thwack that made him howl.

"Now see what you made me do from all your wiggling," she scolded, rubbing his back. "I didn't mean to hurt you. Anyway, if you keep your suit jacket buttoned, maybe no one will notice how low you're wearing your trousers. Wait a minute. Your necktie's crooked."

"I'm late already!" he cried, dancing with impatience. "I'll have to run all the way down to the courthouse, and it's your fault!"

"Thank God your brother Karl never had a mouth on him like you have."

Letting the screen door slam behind him, Hank yelled back, "That's 'cause Karl takes after Pop. I take after *you*!"

As he ran up the path to the back gate, he could hear her rich laughter ringing out from the kitchen. Hank grinned, too. It was true—he and his mother really were alike, and not only in looks.

Even though it was early morning, firecrackers banged in the backyards he passed. The day promised to be muggy. Keeping his suit jacket on would make him uncomfortable, but he had to look nice for the naturalization ceremony. Usually immigrants had to go all the way to Pittsburgh for their citizenship examinations, but because of the war, mill officials wanted to get the greatest number of immigrants naturalized as quickly as possible, believing that if laborers became citizens, they'd work harder for the war effort. Federal judges now traveled from mill town to mill town to expedite the swearing-in, even on the holiday.

"I thought you weren't going to make it," Billy said when Hank ran in, panting. More than two dozen immigrants of all ages crowded the courtroom, all dressed in their best.

"Where should I stand?" Hank asked. "Hello, Zosia. Hello, Mr. Radichevych. My mother and father send congratulations to you on this great occasion."

"Don't say it yet—not till he passes," Billy warned Hank, holding up crossed fingers. "Just in case."

"Should I stand here beside you, Billy? I don't want anybody to think I'm taking the test."

"No one'll think that. Kids under eighteen don't need to take the test—not me, and not Zosia, either, because we become citizens if my father passes. So does my mother. She didn't even bother to come."

From the front of the room a door opened; a judge in a long black robe came up behind the bench. He flapped his arms as if to pull cooler air into his dangling black sleeves.

"Court of the Department of Naturalization is in session," a bailiff intoned. "Judge Morton Malkovitz presiding."

"That's good," Billy whispered to Hank. "He has a foreign name. Maybe he'll be easier."

"Those applying for citizenship, line up in front of the bench," the bailiff instructed.

Only nine men came forward out of the crowd; the rest in the room were family members gathered to witness the event. Everyone seemed happy and excited, except for the nine men in line, who looked nervous. Billy's father stood on the left—if the judge started from that end, he'd be first. He ran his fingers through his thin hair.

"Name," the bailiff said.

"Me? Bogdan Radichevych." Shuffling, he moved forward to hand a paper to the judge.

The judge glanced at it and said, "Mr. Radichevych, it states here that you have completed a course in citizenship preparation."

"Yes, sir." For twenty weeks he'd gone to classes at the library for one hour after the end of day shift, or one hour before the beginning of night shift, whichever he happened to be working.

"Your teacher has written that you read English at the second-grade level. Would you read this aloud?" The judge pointed to a line in a book.

Billy and Zosia tensed as their father strained forward to stare at the page. Sweat stood on his forehead and began to drip off the tip of his nose. "Uh . . ."

"Please hurry, Mr. Radichevych."

"The . . . American . . . flag . . . has . . ." He hesitated, and Billy sucked in his breath. "S . . . seven! . . . red . . . stripes . . . and . . . six . . . white stripes." Fearful, Mr. Radichevych looked up at the judge.

84

"Very good," the judge told him. "Now, name the three branches of the American government."

Mr. Radichevych breathed again. He knew all about that—he'd studied it thoroughly. "Executive—this means president," he said. "Legislative—is American Congress. And judicial—for judge, like you, your honor."

Judge Malkovitz fanned himself with the paper. "You may step back in line," he said, and went on to the next candidate for citizenship.

"Is right, how I answer?" Mr. Radichevych whispered.

"You did fine, Papa. Just fine." Billy and Zosia nodded and squeezed their father's hands. They'd have to wait until all the other candidates had finished, but they were almost certain their father had passed.

When the last man had been tested, the judge said, "I usually make a little speech, but it's too hot. Hot as the Fourth of July, right?" He laughed at his little joke, signaling to the people in the courtroom that it was all right for them to laugh, too—the judge had said something meant to be amusing. "Now! All of you new citizens—yes, you all passed," he told them, "step forward and raise your right hands. Repeat after me." Phrase by phrase he spoke the oath of allegiance to the United States of America.

"I hereby declare an oath . . . that I absolutely and entirely renounce . . . and abjure all allegiance . . . and fidelity . . . to any foreign prince . . . potentate . . . state . . . or sovereignty. . . ."

The phrases were repeated in so many different accents that, put all together, they could hardly be understood. The rhythm was clear, though. Hank saw Billy and Zosia raise their hands to say the oath with their father.

"And I will bear true faith and allegiance. . . ."

Then it was over, and everyone kissed everyone else, even Hank. To escape, he ducked out the door to the sidewalk. When the Radichevych family came out, Hank handed an American flag to each of them.

"Are these the ones from last year?" Billy asked, grinning.

"Yeah. I've been saving them. If your mother'd come today, I wouldn't have had enough."

Zosia put the stem of the flag through a buttonhole of her white blouse. Hank watched, until he realized he was staring intently at a young woman's *chest*. He blushed, looked away, and started to talk too fast. "So I'll meet you after you finish work tonight, Billy, and we'll get to Kennywood Park in time for some rides before the fireworks start after it gets dark."

"Hey, I'll tell you what," Billy said. "If you don't have to go home right away, come on down to the mill with me. I want you to see where I work."

Still flustered about Zosia's figure, Hank stammered, "The mill?"

"Yeah. I want to show you the blower room. My boss won't mind. I'm on his good list today because I gave up the holiday to work—except for this morning. Even Puttkamer—that's my boss—figured it was important for me to come here with my father."

Hank hesitated.

"There's nothing scary about the blower room," Billy said. "There's no fire or anything. Just big machines."

How could he tell Billy that he was afraid to even walk through the mill gate, that he still had dreams the mill was trying to swallow him? But Hank wanted to do what Billy wanted—after all, it was Billy's special day. "Okay," he said reluctantly. "But just for a couple minutes."

After they'd said good-bye to Zosia and Mr. Radichevych, they hurried down Canaan Avenue. "Wait'll you see Puttkamer," Billy said. "Otto Puttkamer. He's *huge*! I bet he weighs three-fifty, maybe four hundred pounds. Wait'll you see him."

"Uh-huh."

"I left my work clothes at work so I wouldn't have to go home to change. I'll just change when I get there. Puttkamer said not to bring my dinner pail today—he's bringing extra food for a treat in honor of my citizenship. He eats so much he usually carries two dinner pails, anyway."

"Uh-huh."

"What if my father hadn't passed? But I knew he would. He studied so hard. I helped him, and Zosia helped him. He can read English pretty good now. Better than it sounded like in the courtroom. He was just scared."

"Uh-huh."

"So now I'm an American, too. If we run into Ralph Qualls and Ernie Ingram at Kennywood Park tonight, we'll punch 'em in the mouth. I'll take Qualls and you take Ingram."

"Uh-huh."

Billy laughed. "Or do you want Qualls?"

"Huh?" Hank looked up at him.

"I knew you weren't listening." Billy rammed his fist into Hank's chest and rotated it like a drill. "I said this is what we're going to do to Qualls and Ingram. I'm an American now, so just let 'em try to call me a dumb Hunkie!"

"Let's just stay out of their way," Hank said. " 'Discretion is the better part of valor.' We had to write that in penmanship class after you quit school."

"What's it mean?"

"It means it's smarter to run away than get the crap kicked out of us by those two ugly goons. Even if you are an American now. Hey, where's the flag I gave you?"

"Zosia took it home for me."

They'd walked through the lower mill gate and were coming close to the blower room. "Hear the noise?" Billy asked. "It ain't scary, but it sure is loud!"

Maybe not scary to *you,* Hank thought.

"Here it is."

The blower-room din was deafening. Twelve-foot-diameter flywheels squealed like wounded banshees as they rotated. Hank stood rooted to the concrete floor, staring up at vertical steam engines, three stories high, that rose from ground level to fifty feet above him. Flights of steel stairs led to catwalks at each of the three levels, with the catwalks on the lowest story rising and descending over the enormous flywheels sunk halfway into the floor.

"What I do," Billy said, shouting over the din, "is keep everything oiled. I go up and down those stairs twenty times a shift so I can squirt oil into the gears and fill the oil cups. You should see—I have to stretch over to reach the oil cups all the way at the top. Once I almost fell."

Hank shuddered.

"But I didn't. See, there's mesh screen all around to keep things from falling off the catwalk. It's *pretty* safe."

Billy's work clothes lay rolled up on a bench. Unself-consciously he took off his good suit and white shirt, handing them to Hank. "Take these up to my house, will you?" he asked. "I don't want to leave them here 'cause they'll get dirty." He shrugged into a gray work shirt and pulled on bib overalls. "Hey, here comes Mr. Puttkamer. Come on, I want you to meet him."

Hank hadn't paid attention earlier when Billy had described Otto Puttkamer. Now the size of the man awed him.

"DID HE MAKE IT?" Puttkamer bellowed to Billy. Years of working in the noise of the blower room had given Puttkamer a voice that could peel rust off the sheet-steel walls.

"Yes," Billy shouted. "My father passed, so now I'm an American."

"GOOD!" Puttkamer roared. "WHO'S THIS?"

"My friend Hank Kerner. His father is Hugo Kerner from the open hearth."

"I KNOW HUGO. HE'S A GOOD MAN. SO HANK WANTS A LOOK AROUND THE BLOWER ROOM?"

Billy nodded and poked Hank until he nodded, too.

"HE CAN STAND OVER THERE WITH ME. WE DON'T WANT NOTHIN' FALLIN' ON HIS HEAD. YOU GET TO WORK, BILLY."

Otto Puttkamer was much like the machines in the blower room. His eyes had sunk into the flesh around them the way bolts were set into concrete. Beneath his ears, his neck swelled like a flange on a section of steam pipe. When he talked—or roared—his little round chin bobbed like a cork in a bucket of oil. His thick shafts of arms swung when he walked ahead of Hank, and his massive behind rocked like the flywheels.

"BILLY'S A GOOD WORKER," Puttkamer roared as they watched Billy scamper up the stairs to the top catwalk, holding an oil can. After a moment, Puttkamer asked, "YOU WANNA GO UP THERE WITH HIM?"

"No!" Hank saw Billy running around the catwalk, not even holding on, leaning over to squirt oil everywhere metal touched metal.

"IT'S AWRIGHT, IF YOU WANNA. I KNOW HOW BOYS LIKE TO CLIMB. GO AHEAD, GO ON UP. GREAT VIEW FROM UP THERE."

Maybe Hank shook his head too vigorously. Puttkamer stared at him with beady brown eyes in which the surprise changed to pity. "OH," was all he said.

Oh—what? That Puttkamer had realized Hank was a sissy-pants afraid to join Billy on a narrow catwalk fifty feet off the ground? Puttkamer looked away.

"Tell Billy I'll see him after work," Hank said hastily, turning to go. He turned back to add, "Please, sir," not wanting to sound bossy to Billy's boss.

"I'LL TELL HIM."

At the door Hank turned around once more. Puttkamer was staring after him.

He crossed the railroad tracks, the quickest way out of the mill yard. Muggy heat pressed down on him along with the falling soot. Deciding he didn't care whether anyone saw that his pants hung too low beneath his crotch, like a circus clown's, he peeled off his suit coat. Past the mill grounds, Hank stopped and leaned against a telegraph pole to consider just how big a coward he actually was.

As the war dragged on—fifteen months now since the United States had entered it—people in Canaan were talking a lot about cowardice. Steelworkers could get an exemption from the draft because steelmaking was an essential war industry. Many of the men took exemptions and stayed in the mill; others enlisted, claiming it was their patriotic duty.

Hank had fought a boy in the school yard for saying that military-age men who stayed in the mill were dirty yellow-bellied slackers. Hank, who always tried to avoid fights, had started this one, and he'd kept fighting till the principal pulled him off the other boy. He'd *had* to fight—after all, his brother Karl was still in the mill. Karl hadn't joined the Army Air Service or anything else.

"Karl isn't yellow," Hank said out loud, and looked around to see if anyone had heard him. People were walking along the sidewalk in little clusters on their way to the Fourth of July parade.

He debated whether to go to the parade. He really didn't want to stand on the curb in too-short pants, holding Billy's good suit in that sweaty, muggy weather, to watch soldiers in uniform march past while everyone cheered. Anyway, he had no one to go with.

The duplex Karl and Margie rented was only a couple of blocks away. Maybe Karl would be home. Karl wasn't yellow—Hank was certain of that. He'd seen him rabbling that furnace full of molten steel, exhilarated by the heat and the danger. Karl was no coward, for sure. And Hank himself wasn't a sissy about *everything,* just about the mill, mostly.

When he climbed the stairs to the narrow wooden porch at Karl's house, he found the door standing open. "Come on in," Karl's voice called, not asking who'd knocked.

The living room was empty. A stillness hung over it as heavy as the heat. Dust motes floated through the light from the window and settled out of sight in the shadows on the floor.

Hank looked into the tiny dining room with its heavy mahogany table. He left his coat and Billy's clothes on the table before he went into the kitchen, where he found Karl sitting on a chair, his shirt unbuttoned and hanging loose, his head in his hands.

"Oh, it's you, Hank," Karl said hoarsely. "I thought it might be Kathleen or Jame."

"What's the matter?" Hank asked. From the way Karl sounded, something must have gone wrong.

Karl swallowed. "Sit down," he said, kicking out another chair. "Margie's upstairs. She's . . ." He got up, went to the sink, and filled a glass with water. "Hot, isn't it? The weather, I mean. Wish we had some lemonade or something I could give you. Want a drink of water? Or . . . or . . . I don't. . . ." He looked at the glass in his hand as though he wondered who'd put it there.

Hank's insides tightened. Whatever had gone wrong must be pretty serious to unsettle Karl that much.

"It's all right," Hank told him. "I'm not thirsty."

Leaning against the sink, Karl said, "I guess you can tell that . . . things aren't normal."

Hank nodded as Karl went back to the chair and sat down again. He stared at Hank for what seemed a long time, although it was probably only a minute, before he said, "We just got word a couple of hours ago. Francis X was killed in action. Shot. At Belleau Wood."

"Oh." At first, Hank felt nothing. It was like reading about some stranger's death in the papers—a death that didn't particularly concern him. Lots of American soldiers were dying in France. Then he remembered that just last summer, he'd stood on the church steps trying on Francis X Culley's army cap, listening to Francis X make machine-gun noises like a little kid.

"Margie's upstairs crying," Karl told him. "It's a good thing I didn't go to work today. I've been putting in so much overtime I decided to go ahead and take the holiday off. Not that I'm doing Margie much good. Hell, I feel terrible that her brother's dead. Absolutely terrible—Francis X was only eighteen!"

Not so long ago, Francis X had been a kid like Hank. Small, too—probably he'd gotten beat up in fights with bigger boys. Maybe he'd been scared by certain things like Hank was.

"But . . ." Karl's voice broke. "Part of the reason I feel so rotten is that—and I'd never say this to anyone but you, Hank—but the truth is . . . I . . . I never liked Francis X."

Hank gasped. Karl had spoken ill about a dead person. You weren't supposed to do that, especially not about an American soldier who'd died for his country.

Karl looked as if he'd been close to crying, or really crying, for quite a while. His eyes were sunken and blood-shot. The words rushed out of him as he went on, "He was my wife's brother, but I couldn't stand him. When he was little he was a pest and a sneak, and when he got older he got even worse. Now, probably, Margie'll want to name the baby after Francis X because he's dead."

"Baby?"

"Yeah. Hardly anyone knows yet. We're going to have a baby in December." Karl swung around and grabbed Hank's hands. "What kind of a terrible person am I?" he cried. "You know what's eating my guts out? First, that Francis X is dead—that's awful enough, even if I didn't like him. Second, that everyone'll call him a hero now."

"Isn't he a hero?" Hank asked. "I mean—wasn't he? He died for his country. He even enlisted when he didn't have to—he told me that himself."

Karl sniffed and rubbed his cheeks. "I'm sweating," he said, but what he wiped away looked more like tears than like the sweat that had dripped from Mr. Radichevych's face in the courtroom. "Hank, I'm going to let you in on something. It's a secret, and I don't want you ever to tell anyone else. Promise?"

"Sure." Hank raised his right hand.

"I shouldn't even say this to you 'cause you're only a kid, but hell, I gotta say it so at least someone understands." Hank waited.

"The only reason Francis X joined the army was to stay out of jail. He got arrested for robbing a drunk behind McToole's Saloon, and the judge said he'd let him off if Francis X enlisted. Then he bragged all over town about how patriotic he was 'cause he'd joined up."

"Does Margie know that?" Hank asked.

"Yeah. The whole Culley family knew, but no one else did. His parents had to sign the consent papers since he was only seventeen when he left."

Karl folded a wrinkled handkerchief and mopped his

forehead. "What hurts like hell is that—well, people on the street look at me funny, or they don't look at me at all—I mean, they intentionally avoid looking at me, like they're disgusted, 'cause I'm some kind of scum. A slacker. But the superintendent himself begged me to stay in the open hearth. He said I was crucial to the operation. You didn't know that, did you?"

Hank shook his head.

"No one does. I don't go around bragging."

"Why not? You ought to tell people."

"Huh! People think what they want to think. And now they'll all think Francis X was a hero. Maybe he was—how do I know? Maybe when he got on the battlefield, he did turn into a hero."

Hank stood up. Awkwardly, he patted Karl's shoulder. "I think you're a hero," he told him.

Karl's arms circled Hank and pulled him forward. He leaned his face against Hank's shirtfront; Hank could feel the dampness from sweat or tears, whichever it was. "You're a good brother," Karl said, his voice muffled. "Tell Mom and Pop the news, will you?"

"About the baby?"

"No, about Francis X. They already know about the baby. I wish I had lemonade or something to give you. . . ."

"It doesn't matter."

"I gotta go up to Margie. Remember—don't ever tell a living soul what I told you. I shouldn't have. . . . but I needed. . . ." He heaved a sigh so deep it was almost a sob.

When Hank left, Karl had started up the stairs to comfort his wife.

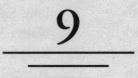

9

August 11, 1918

On the way to the streetcar stop, Hank and Billy detoured to the post office to read the list. Once a week the post-office manager updated the list of men from Canaan who'd been killed in action.

Not much more than a year earlier, the boys had stood only a block from where they were standing now. They'd sung wildly, at the tops of their voices, as the Fourth of July parade passed them, " 'Say a prayer, say a prayer, say a prayer for the boys over there.' " Now Hank was saying that prayer for the names on the list, the ones who wouldn't be back when it was over, over there.

"No new names this week," he said.

"How can you read so fast?" Billy asked him. "I'm just starting the *s*'s."

"I dunno." Hank read the whole list again:

Josef Bienick

Raymond C. Burns

Francis X. Culley

John Dzara

William J. Eadie

Thomas E. Edwards

George N. Gessner

William Carl Goltz

Edward M. Hanson

Joseph Hroziencik

Victor Jones

Albert Linkhauer

Frank E. Lowstetter

Joseph J. Opalka

John C. Palotas

Wladyslaw Rodominski

William A. Schafer

John Snvir

Walter Starzinski

Joseph Suroski

Michael Svec

Anton Swiridenok

Wilbur B. Young

William Hugo Zewe

"There are four Williams and four Josephs," Hank said, "but one of the Josephs is spelled different."

"The Polish way," Billy told him.

"So I guess you could say there are more Williams than any other name, unless you count that different spelling with the Josephs, which would make it a tie."

"And three Johns," Billy said, "and after that there's no more matches."

Hank hitched up the waistband of his new gray pants before they turned to walk down the hill. The pants were a bit too long, but Mr. Levine had said that since Hank had finally started to get taller, better have the cuffs cover the instep of his shoes for a little extra growing room. "You never said if you like my new suit," he told Billy.

"I like it fine."

"It's my birthday present from my mom and pop. The shirt and tie, too."

"You look good," Billy said. "Here's something to go with it. Happy birthday."

They'd reached the streetcar stop when Billy handed Hank the small package. "What is it?" Hank asked, fumbling with the lid.

"You'll see."

Laid diagonally inside, he saw when he opened the box, was a stickpin with a tiny gold eagle at the top.

"It isn't solid gold," Billy said, "but it's gold-plated. Go ahead, stick it in your tie. Want me to do it for you?"

"Yeah. This is swell, Billy. I never had a stickpin before."

"Hold still. Quit wiggling. There! Zosia helped me pick it out. She said a stickpin might be kind of grown-up for a boy's twelfth birthday, but since you've had long pants for so long anyway, you might as well go whole hog."

Now that he was somewhat bigger, Hank hoped people would at least take him for twelve. He got tired of always being mistaken for younger than his real age. Especially since Billy, at fourteen-and-a-half, looked sixteen. Billy's round face had grown leaner, bonier, and his hands had broadened and blunted and were lined with the mill dirt he could never get rid of, no matter how hard he scrubbed.

A newsboy stood at the streetcar stop, shifting from foot to foot, waiting to sell the *Pittsburgh Post-Gazette* to the passengers who would get off the streetcar when it arrived. Hank bent his head to read the front page.

"Look at that headline," he said to Billy. "FIVE AMERICAN AIRMEN FIGHT TWELVE ENEMY AIRPLANES. YANKS SHOOT DOWN TWO."

Every day Hank searched the newspapers for stories about Yankee pilots engaged in dogfights with enemy airmen. Those American fliers were his heroes. Once, for a fleeting moment, he'd wondered if twelve-year-old boys in Germany thought *their* pilots were heroes, too, but that idea was so disloyal that Hank had pushed it right out of his mind.

"You wanna buy a paper?" the newsboy asked hopefully, holding it up.

"Nah. Look, Billy, it says, 'No American casualties.' "

"Yeah. We always kill a lot of Germans, and they hardly ever get any of our guys, from what the papers say. I don't know why the war's lasting so long. If it goes on for two more years, maybe I'll enlist."

"You'd only be sixteen!"

"My parents could sign for me." Then Billy shook his head. "No, they never would. I'm the only son. But maybe . . ."

The streetcar that rumbled up just then wasn't crowded, so both boys got seats. Before long the heat and the rocking had put Billy to sleep. He'd worked until six o'clock the evening before and would report for work at six o'clock that evening. The twenty-four hours off happened every other week, when steelworkers changed from day shift to night shift. On the alternate turnarounds, when they changed from night shift to day shift, they worked twenty-four hours straight through, with no breaks. That was the most dangerous time in the mill, when the greatest number of accidents occurred.

Usually Billy caught up on his sleep during his twenty-four hours off, but because this was Hank's birthday, he'd risen early, attended church, and then met Hank so that they could go to Pittsburgh. Not all the way to Pittsburgh—they'd leave the streetcar at Oakland. They were heading for the Carnegie Museum.

Hank let Billy sleep. Idly, he read the advertisements above the windows of the streetcar, but that took only a few minutes. For miles the streetcar tracks ran past steel mills—Canaan Works, Braddock Works, Homestead Works, all part of United States Steel Corporation, all sending plumes of smoke and steam into the air while railroad cars filled with coal and ore rolled in to feed the mills. Black and orange, Hank thought. Black coal and coke and soot on everything and everyone. Orange ore and smoke and flames and rust. No green for trees or blue for skies, because smoke hid the skies, and trees couldn't stay alive next to steel mills.

"Billy, I think we're getting close," Hank said, shaking his arm. "You better help me figure out the right stop."

"I've never been there, either," Billy said, blinking his eyes as he came awake. "We ought to ask the conductor."

"Two more stops," the conductor told them when Hank asked. To make sure they wouldn't miss it, the boys hung from overhead straps close to the streetcar's front door.

"Carnegie Museum!" the conductor sang out. "Right over there across the street, fellas."

From the curb, Billy exclaimed, "It's lots bigger than the library in Canaan. I didn't think it would be that big."

"Me, either. It's like a palace."

Weeks before, when they'd figured out that Hank's birthday would fall on one of Billy's work-free Sundays, they'd discussed different ways to celebrate it. The movies.

A picnic. Swimming in the river. The penny arcade at Kennywood Park, where they could maybe win a celluloid doll by knocking down milk bottles with baseballs. But what would they do with a celluloid doll if they won one?

Then Hank thought about his teacher, Miss Burrus, who'd been appalled to learn that not a single student in the entire seventh grade had ever visited the Carnegie Museum. "It's a treasure!" she'd exclaimed. "Art and exhibits from all over the world! The American Indian exhibit by itself is worth the trip, not to mention all the other wonderful things there."

She'd gone on to tell them about some of the other wonderful things, and one in particular had caught Hank's attention. So when Billy said he'd do whatever Hank decided, Hank chose the Carnegie Museum.

And there it was, right in front of them, an enormous gray sandstone building with two towers at one end. They had to wait for another streetcar to pass before they could run across Forbes Street. At the front of the building they reached stairs that led through a triple-arched entranceway onto marble floors. "How do we know where to go to see what we want to see?" Billy whispered.

"Ask somebody, I guess."

Barely moving his hand so that he wouldn't appear ill-mannered, Billy pointed to a guard. "Him?"

"Okay. Sir," Hank inquired, "where can we find the live dinosaur skeleton?"

The guard smirked. "I never heard of any kind of skeleton being alive, sonny. But go straight ahead, make a left through the marine hall, and you'll see it. Can't miss it, in fact."

Hank blushed. Of course he knew the dinosaur wasn't alive—he meant that it had been, once. The skeleton was honest-to-gosh dinosaur bone, Miss Burrus had told the seventh graders. Not a fake plaster cast, but real bone. Fossilized.

They walked, wanting to run through the halls but realizing that in an imposing public building like this one, even young boys were supposed to behave with decorum. Especially young boys. "Marine hall?" Billy whispered. "Do they have an army hall and a navy hall, too?"

Hank didn't have to answer because they'd reached the marine hall, which was filled with exhibits of fish and other sea creatures, some quite strange-looking.

"Don't slow down—I think we're coming to the dinosaur. It should be in the next room," Hank said. His excitement mounted, but nothing—no book-knowledge, no teacher's description—could have prepared him for his first sight of the skeleton.

Eighty-four feet long from the nose of its small skull to the tip of its massive tail, the fossil was so gargantuan that its heavy bones had to be held upright by thick steel rods. Billy and Hank walked all the way around it, twice, just absorbing the idea that a creature like that could ever have moved on the earth. Then they stopped, ready for a closer, bone-by-bone examination.

"It's . . . it's . . . terrific!" Billy couldn't manage more.

"*Diplodocus*," Hank murmured.

"Huh?"

"*Diplodocus carnegii*. That's its name."

"How do you know?"

"It says so on that sign right there." Hank pointed. "See?

The bones got excavated at a place called Sheep Creek, Wyoming, and then the whole thing was shipped here in pieces and they put it together. Why'd we wait so long to come see it?"

" 'Cause we didn't know."

For a half hour they moved from one part to another of the skeleton, discussing the crescendo of ribs, the hipbones that reached fifteen feet above the floor, and each verte-bra—they counted them twice, debating where the tail began. Another skeleton stood beside *Diplodocus,* but that one was not as enormous and it had no head, so the boys considered it less satisfying. *Diplodocus* was perfect.

"This was worth seeing," Billy said solemnly. "Really. I don't care if it did take us an hour and a half to get here and it's gonna take another hour and a half to get home. It's been worth it. But we better find out what time it is right now, because I need to be back in Canaan by five, at the latest, so I can go home and change into my work clothes and get to work by six."

"Maybe the guard out front has a watch," Hank suggested, "or maybe there's a clock somewhere."

Trying to retrace their way to the front door where the guard was, they passed through a massively high room with a skylight in the domed ceiling. Hank stopped dead, in the middle of the floor. Hazy radiance from the skylight settled on chalk white figures standing against the walls, some in rigid postures, others turned, knees bent, their arms pointing or outstretched.

"Look!" Hank whispered so low that Billy couldn't hear. "What?"

"Look at that!"

Slowly, they moved forward until they stood in the west aisle, at the pedestal of a tall statue. THE VENUS OF MELOS, APHRODITE, a sign said. GREEK, FOURTH CENTURY B.C. FOUND, 1820, ISLAND OF MELOS. ORIGINAL IN LOUVRE.

The top of the statue's pedestal was at a level with Hank's chest. His eyes, if he held them straight ahead, connected somewhere beneath her knees, at about midshin. He tilted back his head, raising his unblinking gaze inch by inch up the smooth white statue, past the place where the bed sheet or whatever it was hung so low on her hips that if she were real it would have dropped off, past the depression for the belly button—or did they call it something else in the fourth century B.C.? Up past the waist, to . . .

"Wow!" he whispered, and beside him, Billy nodded. Hank's fingertips twitched, wanting to touch that part of the stark white body, which had to be rigid since it was a statue, but looked so smooth and inviting. But it was too high, it was out of his reach, and anyway, signs all over the place warned, DO NOT TOUCH THE EXHIBITS!

It took a minute for him to notice that she had no arms. That she possessed a head was of fleeting interest; his gaze darted back to those perfect, rounded. . . .

"There's other ones," Billy whispered. "Up there."

"Other ones?"

"Other statues. Totally naked."

But the other ones were too elevated to get a good look at. From where the boys stood, they could stare seventy feet straight up to the skylight, but at the level of the second floor, a balcony with a railing edged the vast cube of empty space. At intervals, the railing was interrupted by pedestals, which held other statues—gods and athletes and goddesses draped in sculptured robes from shoulder to toe. Two of the goddesses, though, appeared to be altogether nude.

"How do we get up there?" Hank whispered.

"There's some stairs over there," Billy answered. "Wait, Hank—what time is it?"

"Let's find a clock," Hank muttered, and this time the boys didn't worry about decorum as they rushed through the imposing halls to find the guard at the front door.

"Three-thirty," the guard told them.

"We gotta go right now," Billy said. "I'm sorry."

Hank turned stricken eyes to his friend. "Just ten more minutes?"

"Sorry," Billy repeated apologetically. "We can come back on my next day off, though."

Two weeks to wait before they could explore the second-story balcony! For a fleeting instant Hank considered sending Billy home without him, but that wouldn't be right. Billy probably wanted to see those statues as badly as Hank did. It would be only fair to wait until they could see them together.

Just before the streetcar came they found a pushcart vendor and bought hot dogs; Billy insisted on paying for them, since it was Hank's birthday. Holding one in each hand, they boarded the streetcar and found a seat in the back. "Grab that newspaper," Hank said, gesturing toward a *Pittsburgh Sun-Telegraph* someone had left behind. Carefully, they spread the newspaper on their laps so that they wouldn't spill mustard on their good suits.

106

Hank looked at the headline: SOMME SALIENT SMASHED; 400 GUNS AND 24,000 MEN CAPTURED. A smaller headline reported, ALLIED SOLDIERS BOMBARDED WITH POISON GAS. But Hank didn't want to read about the war—he didn't even want to think about it just then.

"This has been some day," Billy said.

"Yeah!" Hank finished his second hot dog and wiped his hands on his pocket handkerchief. "You're sure we can come back again in two weeks?"

"I think so. What did you like best?" Billy asked.

"Well, the dinosaur was great. But what did I like best? Two things. Two really knockout things. And they weren't on the dinosaur." Hank and Billy burst out laughing, poking each other and rolling their eyes, which was all right because they were in the back of the streetcar pretty much by themselves, and no one would have known what they were laughing about, anyway.

Billy leaned close to Hank and spoke very softly. "They don't really look like that. Real ones don't."

"What are you talking about? Did you ever see . . . ?"

"Yeah."

"A naked woman? Honest? I don't believe you!"

"It's true." Billy never lied.

"Who?"

"My sister. By accident."

"Oh. You mean when you were little kids," Hank said. That wouldn't really count.

"No, just last Christmas. I went upstairs to clean the ashes out of the coal stove in my parents' bedroom. My mother told me to. Only we didn't know Zosia had gone in there with a basin of water to give herself a bath—'cause

107

it was warmer in there, you know? I walked in on her, and she was naked."

Hank swallowed. Zosia Radichevych, one of the loveliest young women in Canaan, with nothing on. It was more than he could stand to imagine.

"What was it like?" he breathed.

Billy leaned even closer and whispered into Hank's ear, "The most beautiful thing I ever saw in my whole life. Not stiff and white like those statues. Soft, and pink. I . . . I shouldn't say any more. After all, she's my sister."

Hank desperately wanted to know more, but how could he insist? She was, as Billy had said, his sister. "What'd she do when you busted in on her?" he asked.

"She was nice about it. She didn't yell or scream or anything; she just told me to get out of there fast and close the door before Mama or Papa came upstairs. She knew I didn't do it on purpose."

Hank let out his breath and leaned back against the seat. He'd never in his life seen uncovered female flesh. Each time his sister Kathleen had nursed her babies, Hank's mother always made him leave the room.

"When I get married," Billy said, "I hope my wife will look as beautiful as Zosia did that day."

"Married!"

"Yeah. In four or five years."

"Four or five years!"

"You sound like an echo," Billy said. "Your brother Karl was twenty when he got married. I'll be twenty in five and a half years, but I probably won't wait that long if I have a good job. A man at our church already tried to arrange a marriage between me and his daughter, but my father said no, that this is America and I get to pick my own wife when I'm ready."

Shocked, Hank stared open-mouthed at Billy. How could Billy even talk about such a thing as marriage, when Hank's most pressing problem was to persuade his mother to let him wear long pants when he started eighth grade next month?

"I think I already know who I might pick," Billy went on, unmindful of Hank's chagrin. "There's this girl at church—her name is Marya Popovich. She's maybe not as pretty as Zosia, but she's real nice, and she's smart in school like you, Hank. She's already in high school. But who knows? Maybe someone else'll come along before I decide."

Hank turned away and pressed his face against the window. Something had happened between him and Billy. They were getting too different. It had started when Billy went to work in the mill, in a man's job. Now, just seven months later, he was talking about going off to war, if the war lasted long enough. He'd admitted to seeing a woman's naked body, even if it was only his sister. He'd discussed marriage, and not just as a joke, the way they'd once snickered in furtive whispers about what married people did together. Billy had been speaking seriously. And a man Hank didn't know had tried to get Billy engaged to his daughter. But Billy liked a different girl, someone else Hank didn't know. How had all these things happened?

The streetcar jerked along the tracks and Hank's forehead bumped the grimy pane. Being twelve years old, he decided, didn't amount to a whole heck of a lot after all.

10

All the mill whistles blew at once, shortly after three in the morning. They didn't stop for half an hour. Within minutes after they began, the pealing of the steeple bell in the Russian Orthodox church—the church on the hill closest to the Kerner house—awakened Hank.

"What's going on?" he asked, stumbling into the hall that separated his room from his parents'.

"They signed the armistice, I guess," his father answered. Hugo Kerner stood in his nightshirt, barefoot. Dim light from the top of the stairwell cast odd shadows under the knobby veins on his legs. "To end the war."

"They signed it in the middle of the night?" Hank wondered. "No, wait, that's right," he corrected himself, coming more awake. "It wouldn't be the middle of the night in France, would it?"

"No, it will end in the morning over there," his father answered. "The eleventh hour of the eleventh day of the eleventh month. Imagine that!"

"The war's over, then, at last," Maggie Rose said. "Thank God. Let's all get back to bed before we freeze."

In his room, Hank settled himself under the quilt to think about the war being over. He knew he would remember this moment all his life. It was probably the most important event he'd ever lived through, this ending of the war that would end all wars and make the world safe for democracy. But he fell asleep again too quickly, before he could put together any thoughts important enough to last a lifetime.

When he reached school that morning, the eighth graders from Miss Wagstaff's room had gathered in small clusters. At a glance Hank saw that at least half a dozen classmates hadn't come to school. There'd been talk of closing the schools because of the epidemic of Spanish influenza, but the city council hadn't acted on the talk one way or another, so the schools had stayed open. On this day, Monday, November 11, seven eighth graders were absent. But maybe they'd just stayed home believing that because of the armistice, school would be called off.

"It's over, huh?" Hank said, edging toward one of the huddled bands of classmates.

"Yeah." Even on this most important day, he felt their exclusion. Since Billy quit school, Hank had been the class loner. At recess the boys chose teams without him, and the girls ignored him always, except when they called him Baby Hank—even though he'd grown taller, he was far from catching up to the heights of his classmates. The boys who still wore knickers hated Hank for his long pants, and a lot of the others hated him for being the smartest in the class. Sometimes he tried to act friendly, knowing it never did much good. Mostly he stayed by himself.

"You think they'll let us out early?" he asked a boy standing beside another group.

"How should I know? I'm not the principal."

In spite of the jubilant news that the armistice had been signed just six hours earlier, the students seemed oddly subdued. Then Hank looked at the teacher, and understood.

Miss Wagstaff sat stiffly at her desk, her fingers laced pale-knuckled in front of her as she stared unseeing. Tears coursed down her cheeks. Behind her, someone had written in yellow chalk on the blackboard, WAR'S OVER! WE WON! HOORAY!

Everyone in the class knew why Miss Wagstaff was crying. Dorie Wunderly had heard the other teachers talking about it in the halls, and had duly reported it to the kids in the class, who'd whispered the news so often that even Hank had heard it. Weeks before, Miss Wagstaff's fiancé had died in the battle of the Meuse-Argonne. Miss Wagstaff, already thirty years old, would probably never find another man to marry, Dorie had declared.

Someone came into the room with a note from the principal. "Read it out loud, will you, Henry?" Miss Wagstaff asked Hank, her voice husky, her eyes lowered.

"In honor of the signing of the armistice signaling the end of the Great War," Hank read, "school will be dismissed at noon today and will resume tomorrow at the usual hour."

The cheers were halfhearted; how could they rejoice when Miss Wagstaff wept right in front of everyone like that? Eventually, without being told, the students returned to their desks and drew pictures of American flags, or of German airplanes shot down in flames. Dove Wunderly drew a ship full of returning American soldiers, all smiles. Hank read a library book until the bell rang at noon. Miss Wagstaff never spoke another word all morning.

When Hank left school, the sky was so dark with mill smoke it looked like night. Freezing rain had begun to fall; crossing the brick-paved streets became treacherous. Other kids laughed and grabbed one another as they fought to stay upright. Hank skidded and clutched his books.

He avoided sidewalks except where they'd been spread with ashes from coal stoves, some still a little warm underfoot. Since it was safer to walk on dirt, most of the way home he tramped through people's backyards. To get up Pine Alley, he had to grab fence posts and drag himself uphill. Sleet dripped off the brim of his cap, ran down the collar of his coat, and froze the hand he used to grip the railings. The other hand he held inside his coat, pressing his books against his chest to keep them dry.

When he reached his own back gate, he felt half frozen. The glow of light from the kitchen window lured him with the promise that his mother would fuss over him as she helped him out of his wet coat, while somehow at the same time she'd be slipping a pan of milk onto the stove to make

114

him cocoa. But when he got to the back porch, he noticed the coal scuttle lying on its side, with lumps of coal spilled all over the porch.

"Mom?" he called, opening the door.

"She isn't here."

Margie, Karl's wife, sat on the edge of one of the kitchen chairs, her very pregnant torso held peculiarly, as though she were arching herself backward. She smiled at Hank, but the smile looked unnatural, a bit sheepish, or even apologetic. "I've been here since before the storm started," she said. "Your mother went to the parade. Then she was going to buy flannel so we could hem baby diapers, but the storm caught her. She stopped at Kathleen's to wait it out, and phoned from there to let me know."

"There's coal all over the porch. What happened?" Hank asked.

Margie's smile became even more crooked. "I wanted to get more coal from the shed before the yard became too slippery. But it wasn't the yard that was treacherous— it was the porch!"

"You fell?"

"Uh-huh. About an hour ago, I think."

"Did you hurt yourself?" he asked.

"I fell on my back." The smile became a grimace. "These awful pains started. They die down, but they come again."

Hank set his books on the kitchen table and went to crank up the phone on the wall. "I better call somebody to help you," he said. "Mom, or Karl, or a doctor if your back's really—"

"The phone's dead," she told him. "It's been dead since

your mother called. I guess the ice knocked the lines down."

Hank was glad he hadn't bothered to take off his coat and cap. "I'll go get one of the neighbor ladies to help you," he said.

Her hand reached out in a gesture that was both a plea and a command. "Don't leave me, Hank! There's no one around." As she spoke, her breath came in little gasps. "I looked through . . . the windows . . . on all sides of the house. All the neighbor houses are dark. No one's home anywhere."

"Margie, you seem like you're really hurting," Hank protested. "I'll just go from house to house till I find somebody at home. Then I'll bring them here."

"No!" She shook her head vehemently. "You can't leave me! Not now. The baby's coming, I'm pretty sure."

"Huh!" When the meaning of her words hit him, Hank began to shake. "*Your* baby? Now? It's not supposed to come now."

"I know," she panted. "It's early. If . . . if you try to go for help . . . it might happen while you're gone. Ooh . . . this pain's a bad one."

"What'll I do?" he squeaked, wanting his mother, wanting hot cocoa, wanting Margie to be anywhere but here, wanting none of this to be happening.

Her panting slowed after a bit, and Margie breathed more easily. "First," she said, "you probably ought to take your coat off."

Fear filled him, so he rushed around. "I'm going out to pick up the spilled coal," he announced, and kept telling

Margie each thing he did as though she weren't sitting right there to see him. "I'm putting the coal in the stove to build up the fire so it'll be nice and warm for the . . . for you, Margie." He couldn't bring himself to say "baby." Surely someone would get there before Margie gave birth.

"We'll need towels to wrap it in," she told him, her face beginning to tighten again with pain.

"On the clothesline in the cellar. I'm going down right now to get them," Hank announced, and clattered down the steps into the gloomy, dugout, dirt-floor basement. He ran back up to the kitchen with half a dozen towels in his arms, telling Margie, "They're still kind of damp. I'll hang them over the backs of the chairs to dry." Rushing, he picked up every kitchen chair, except the one Margie was sitting on, and shoved them all as close to the stove as he could get them. After draping the chair backs with the towels, he exclaimed, "There! That ought to do it," and rushed to the window to see if anyone was coming. Anyone!

"Hank, I think I ought to lie down," Margie said.

"Where? Upstairs in Mom and Pop's bed?"

"I doubt that I can make it up the stairs," she told him. "When I fell, I really hurt my back."

"I could bring blankets and stuff and put them right here on the floor," he stuttered, but even with blankets on it, the floor would be cold. "Wait! The kitchen table. I'll roll it over here by the stove."

The wheels on the bottom of the table legs squealed as he pushed it, and at the same time, Margie groaned. "How am I going to get up on that table?" she asked Hank.

"I can lower it! See? The wheels'll just slip out of the bottom of each leg. They're not glued or nailed or anything." He demonstrated, lifting the table by each corner in turn; the wheels came off easily. "Now I'll go get some pillows and blankets for you so it won't feel so hard when you lie on it."

This time he flew up the stairs to the second floor, where he stripped his own bed and his parents' bed of every bit of covering. Back in the kitchen, he spread the sheets and blankets carefully on the kitchen table.

Except for the part of her where the baby was, Margie wasn't especially heavy, and Hank's strength seemed to have doubled. As gently as he could, he helped her sit on the edge of the table, then supported her as she lay backward, but she cried out with pain. Hank wanted to cry, too.

"I'm going out on the porch," he said after she was settled. "Karl might be coming."

"He won't come here—he'll go to our house. And not till after six this evening," she said. "After work."

"Maybe my mom's coming. The weather might be clearing up. I'll go look." He had to get out of there, if only for a minute, before Margie shrieked again. From the way her face had begun to contort, another scream appeared close.

Outside, each twig on each tree was sheathed with glassy ice. Crystals of ice seemed to hang in the air, catching an orange aura from the flames of the Bessemer furnace. Except for the perpetual mill sounds—the clang of freight cars coupling, the scrape of charger boxes climbing inclines

118

to load blast furnaces, the grind of cranes crawling on overhead trolleys to pick up hundred-ton ladles of molten steel, sounds that could be heard everywhere in Canaan—the neighborhood was as still as an empty church. All the men were at work, and the women—where were they? Probably, like his mother, they'd gone to the parade and got caught by the storm, so they were now huddled inside the stores down-street, examining merchandise as they waited for a way to get home.

Indignation filled him. A parade—why hadn't the principal announced it? Or maybe all the other kids knew about it, but no one had bothered to tell Hank.

Through the door, he heard Margie cry out again. Frantic, Hank ran to the end of the yard, tramping down the dead stalks of his mother's summer flowers because the garden provided the best traction underfoot. Up and down the alley, every house looked dark. The power—had it gone out, too, to make all the houses dark? No, it was just that no one was home anywhere, because in his own kitchen, the light still shone—he could see it through the window. But if the telephone lines were down, the electric lines might be next. The sky was by now so black with storm that if the lights went out, Margie's baby would be born in darkness.

He ran back to the house, skidding on the porch boards and nearly falling as he flung open the door. Margie lay on the table, blanched, groaning. . . .

"Gotta get something!" Hank cried. Once again, he hurried down to the cellar dugout. In a box in the corner he found all the old oil lamps they'd used before the house was wired for electricity. The lamp chimneys clattered as he carried the box upstairs, set them on the floor, and began to put them together. They were dusty and still sooty; his hands became black; Margie cried out with another pain. Under the sink, Hank found a can of oil. He filled the lamps and lit them, all six, and placed them on the kitchen shelves. Their glow softened the more brittle light from the forty-watt bulbs overhead.

"Hank, you have to help me," Margie cried. "I can't raise my head to see what's happening. My back's too sore."

"What do you want me to do?"

"Wash yourself. You're all dirty from the lamps."

He ripped off his soiled shirt—his undershirt was still clean—and scrubbed his hands and arms at the kitchen sink with yellow laundry soap. "Now what?" he asked.

"If only I could lift my head to see!"

"Let me help." Hank tried to raise Margie by the shoulders, but she screamed again—the scream sent stabs down his spine. "What is it you want to see?" he asked, not understanding.

"Down there. Where the baby's coming out."

Down there! Waves of agitation radiated through him. If Margie couldn't move, couldn't see, would Hank have to . . . ?

"Wait! Wait!" He pulled down the mirror that hung over the kitchen sink. "If I held this . . . down there . . . could you see?"

"Maybe." When she lifted away the sheet that covered her, Hank closed his eyes.

He stood at the foot of the table, head averted, eyes

squeezed shut, following Margie's directions about tilting the mirror—down a little, forward, more to the left, that's it—wincing every time she yelled in pain, not knowing how much time was passing, just that eventually his arms became tired from the heavy weight of the mirror.

Her yells got louder and came oftener until they'd become one continuous, hoarse scream. No longer could he keep his eyes closed—something terrible must be happening! He put down the mirror, and looked at her.

Margie's were the first woman's thighs Hank had ever seen. The sight of them slammed against his senses, but only briefly. Her intimate flesh—the part of the statues he and Billy had found so fascinating the three times they'd gone to the Carnegie Museum—was stretched into a wreath that circled a smeary, blood-streaked, bulging, infant-size skull.

It didn't matter that Margie was a woman and Hank was seeing her uncovered. She needed his help. They both needed him—Margie and the baby whose head was just beginning to show. He reached toward it, and the baby squeezed out some more. Margie kept screaming, but Hank ignored the screams, because that flattened white face was coming into his hands. And then the rest of it, the whole head, and a tiny, perfect body, the skin blue-white. After the feet emerged, he let the baby lie on the sheet between her legs.

"No! Pick it up!" Margie cried. "I have to see—a boy! Hold him up, Hank. Not like that—upside down! He needs to cry so he'll breathe!"

The baby was slippery; Hank was afraid to lift him.

"Bring him to me!" Margie cried, and she began to smack the tiny back as Hank held the infant by the legs.

"Why isn't he crying? He should be crying!" she shrieked. "He's dead! Oh God, he's dead!"

Hank turned as white as the baby, as the limp little body he still held head-down. Dead. All that, all that effort, and it had been born dead.

"Baptize him!" Margie wailed, near hysterics. "At least he can be baptized and go to heaven."

Hank's hands shook; he laid the baby on the table and went to the sink for a glass of water, but how could he hold on to the slippery little dead body and pour water over its head at the same time? He picked up one of the towels that had been drying over the back of a chair; it was rough and scratchy and hot enough that it had a slightly scorched smell, but what did that matter? He wrapped the towel around the baby's body, leaving room for the umbilical cord that still connected it to its mother. Pouring a little water over the baby's head, Hank recited the words every Catholic child learned in catechism class so that they would be prepared for just such an emergency as this. "I baptize you in the name of the Father and the Son and the Holy Ghost. . . ."

What name? he wondered. He couldn't ask Margie because she was sobbing so hard. What did it matter what he was baptized—the little dead baby? Why not Francis X? No, Karl didn't want that. "William . . . Joseph . . . Kerner," Hank decided. William and Joseph for the names on the list of Canaan war heroes, all those dead soldiers who were already in heaven, where the baby would go, too, now that he was baptized. The towel felt very warm in Karl's arms, the water in the glass was cold, but the poor dead infant couldn't feel either of them.

Suddenly, the tiny fingers splayed open, startling Hank so much that he nearly dropped the glass. He peered at the face; it was no longer so white. Hank grabbed the towel-wrapped baby and lifted it upright, toward the light. It wasn't his imagination—the skin color had turned pink. Not just pink—red! The mouth opened, and a raspy sound came out.

Never, for as long as he lived, would Hank forget the look on Margie's face. Joy, of course, but the word was too feeble to describe her when she heard the faint, hoarse cry. Radiance. Rapture. She held out her arms, and Hank laid the baby into them. Time began to move forward again; in just a few minutes, it seemed, Hank's mother came through the front door, exclaiming about the sleet.

Instantly, Maggie Rose took in the scene, took off her coat, and took charge. Hank was dismissed. Up the stairs, in his room, on his bare mattress, he lay facedown and wept, because it had all been too much for a twelve-year-old boy. Too awful, and too wonderful, almost, to bear.

That evening, in Billy's bedroom, Hank's words tumbled out in a swift tangle, because there was so much to tell. "I didn't even think about it when I baptized him William," he said, "that he'll probably be called Billy, just like you."

As Billy coughed, the covers rose and fell on his chest. "He'll be a real Billy," he said. "I'm Bazyli."

"I always thought you liked to be called Billy," Hank said.

"I didn't mind. But Bazyli is who I am."

So Bazyli Radichevych had accepted the name Billy the way he accepted everything—with grace and patience. Hank paused to consider that for an instant, but there was so much more to tell that he had to keep going. "It was . . . it was just . . . I can't explain it. But I decided what I'm gonna be. Want to guess?"

Billy coughed again, then smiled. "Tell me."

"A doctor. I don't care how long it takes. I'll even work in the mill if I have to, to get enough money to go to medical college. If I was a doctor right now, I could give you medicine for that cough."

At the front door, Zosia Radichevych had tried to keep Hank from seeing Billy. "He's really sick," she'd said.

"I'll only stay a couple of minutes," Hank had argued. "There's something really important I have to tell him about."

"Don't let him talk too much," Zosia had warned. "Talking makes him cough."

Now Billy was saying, "I guess the Ukrainian women made enough *pysansky* this year."

"Easter eggs?" Hank asked. "What's that got to do with anything?"

Billy coughed. "The evil monster . . ." He coughed again. Hank saw a glass of water sitting on the table near Billy's bed; he helped Billy drink from it. It seemed to soothe him.

"The evil monster," Billy went on, "is back in his chains. He must be. The war's over, and Margie's baby lived."

"Yeah, I guess so," Hank muttered, too full of his own excitement to worry about Ukrainian fairy tales.

"Only . . ." Billy added. His hoarse voice sounded deep as a grown man's.

"Only what?"

"I didn't tell you. Puttkamer died. You know, my boss?"

"He did?"

"Last week." The blankets quivered as Billy tried to hold back a cough. "That big man. From influenza."

"When I'm a doctor," Hank said, "I'll save lives. People like Puttkamer." His attention was caught by an object on a shelf above Billy's bed. Standing next to a crucifix—the Russian kind, with three crossbars—a clear, amber-colored vase had been half filled with sand to hold, upright, the stems of three small American flags.

"Are those the ones I gave you on your citizenship day?" Hank asked, pointing.

Billy nodded, and coughed so hard Hank could barely make out the words, "Kennywood Park," and "McToole's Saloon."

Zosia came into the room then, her face drawn with concern. "You'll have to go now, Hank," she said. "Bazyli's too sick for company."

"Okay. Stop down at the house as soon as you get better," Hank told his friend. "We'll go see the new Billy."

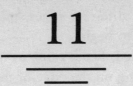

11

November 18, 1918

Scorched with fever. Wracked with cough.

The bell from the Russian Orthodox church rammed through Hank's ears to torment his brain. His brain, sick as it was, could still count the dreadfully slow peals . . . eight, nine, ten, eleven, twelve, thirteen, fourteen. . . .

Silence. "NO!" Hank screamed, or thought he screamed. The death knell always tolled the exact number of years the dead person had spent on earth. Now, after fourteen peals . . . silence.

He willed the pealing to go on. But it had stopped. The stillness pressed heavily against the windows, against the walls, against Hank, crushing him. "NO!" he screamed again, and this time it must have been aloud, because his mother came running. By the time she reached him, he lay unconscious in his bed.

The bells rang in different patterns of peals so that people could know what they were announcing. Rapid pealing, with bells of two different tones, meant that a church service was about to begin.

The room whirled; Hank clung to the bedpost to stay upright. Even sitting on the edge of the bed, he'd barely been able to pull on his long trousers, and he'd missed some of the buttons on his shirt. Standing, he struggled with his suit jacket.

Quiet. He had to stay quiet so his mother couldn't hear him. If she did, she'd never let him go to the funeral.

He knew it was Billy's funeral the bells pealed for. Three days before, the death knell had tolled for Billy. Now it was the funeral knell.

Shoes. Overcoat. Cap. Keep it quiet. No floorboards squeaking. Raise the window inch by inch. Cold wind blew in, clearing Hank's burning head. Snow, snow everywhere, coming into the room with him, melting on his skin, while outside it purified Canaan.

His bedroom window was right above the kitchen window. If his mother happened to be in the kitchen, she'd see him drop. He hoped she was in her bed, resting after all the nights she'd sat up with him while he coughed until there was no more breath in him. During those nights, she said things to his father that she thought Hank couldn't hear, things about Billy Radichevych. And Hank's father would answer sadly, then cross the hall to lower his heavy body into his bed, making the springs squeak. Sleep, work, eat, sleep, work again. Steelworkers never stopped, because steel mills never stopped.

One leg out. Onto the ledge above the kitchen window. The other leg out. Quiet. Now . . . let go! He dropped into the deep snow, silently.

Up the hill to the Russian Orthodox church, his head as light as the smoke from the mill, spinning the way the snowflakes spun, blown helter-skelter by the wind. The Russian church had two onion-shaped steeples, one in front and the other in back, both with triple-barred crosses on the top. No one waited outside.

He entered the church and stood in the back. All his senses throbbed with pain. The mournful singing of the cantor and the congregation's responses rumbled through his ears like blower-room noises. Incense, wafting from a censor swung by the priest—Hank remembered him, that priest, with his long black hair parted in the middle—seared Hank's nostrils till he gasped for breath. At the front of the church, a hundred candle flames reflected brilliantly in the gilded holy pictures, stabbing his eyes. From the onion-shaped steeples the bells pealed, booming between Hank's temples as though his skull were a barrel. His knees buckled, but there were no benches to sit on. Everyone in the church was standing.

At the front of the altar rose an icon screen painted with pictures of saints, and in front of the icon screen lay Billy, inside an open coffin.

He was all dressed up in a new dark suit, a lily in his lapel, a cross in his hands. The priest must have been calling him to wake up, because Hank heard the name *Bazyli* repeated again and again. "Call him Billy," Hank said, "and maybe he'll answer you." But no one paid attention to Hank, because everyone was singing too loudly to hear him.

Above Billy, the painted saints wore clothes the colors of jewels, but their faces and bodies looked flat, not round like the statues in the Carnegie Museum, which had seemed more real even though they were all white. And Billy was all white, his face no longer apple-cheeked, but as ashen as the face of the discus thrower in the museum. "Bazyli," the priest chanted, but the people didn't say it right; they sang "*Hospodi pomiloi,*" which was certainly not Billy's name. "Radichevych," Hank told them. "But I always called him Billy Radish."

Then, at the front of the church, people approached the coffin, crossing themselves in that backward way, and leaned over—to do what? Hank couldn't tell. Soon everyone had moved into a line inching forward toward the altar. Curious, Hank went with them, floating, not feeling his feet against the floorboards. When he got to the front, to the foot of the altar, he intended to ask Billy what it was all about, but the line seemed to take forever—it moved ahead at a snail's pace. He smiled, because the saints in the pictures above the altar had turned into statues—of Apollo, of the Standing Diskobolos, of lovely Venus Genetrix, of Athena, Theseus, Demeter, Persephone, and the other milk white Greeks Hank and Billy had come to know so well at the museum. And yet the line of people—men in damp overcoats, women with scarves covering their heads and pulled down over their foreheads—shuffled ahead, not even looking up at the statues that were so young and beautiful, those heroes and athletes as pure as the snow outside.

At last Hank got close enough to see what the people were doing. They were leaning over to kiss Billy's white hand, or to kiss the cross he held upright. If Billy were awake, he certainly wouldn't want that sort of thing going on.

But when Hank reached the coffin, he saw that Billy wasn't asleep at all. Billy was made of marble, just like the statues. Beautiful, cold, dead marble.

Dazed, burning with fever, Hank stood rigid beside the coffin, next to Billy's weeping parents and his sister Zosia. Someone—an usher or a church official—tried to lead him back into the congregation, but Mr. Radichevych shook his head to indicate that it was all right for Hank to stay there. His hand on Hank's arm helped Hank struggle back into his senses, to the feel of his feet on the floor and the remembrance of where he was and why he'd come there.

After the lid of the coffin had been closed, six men took their places around it to carry it outside. As they started, Hank slipped between two of them and rested his hand on the smooth wood. Too sick to help carry Billy, he would at least walk beside his friend for as long as his strength lasted.

12

New Year's Day, 1919

"It's a miracle you're alive, as sick as you were," Margie said.
"That day—going all the way up to the Russian church in
the snow, and then. . . . I'll never understand why you did
such a thing."

"Listen to her," Karl said. "She's starting to sound like
all mothers. I understand, Hank," he said, gripping Hank's
blanket-covered knee. "I'd have done the same thing if it
had been my best friend."

Margie frowned and remarked, "Men! Maybe I should
have had a daughter instead of a son." Then she clutched
the baby against her to convince the Fates she'd only been
joking.

Walking beside Billy's coffin into the snow, Hank had
collapsed on the church steps. He was lifted into the automobile of Yulyona Bonner, the wife of the general

superintendent of the Canaan Works; she'd also been at Billy's funeral. A chauffeur drove them away in the sleek, fancy motorcar, along the snow-slick streets to the Kerner house, while Yulyona Bonner sat in the backseat beside Hank, rubbing his hands. He became conscious slowly, but his thoughts had stayed thick and tangled.

"I'm going to be a doctor," he'd blurted to Mrs. Bonner. "I've got to make this dying stop. There's no good way to die—death is awful! I hate it!"

She'd released his hands. "You can't make dying stop, Hank. If people live, they're going to die. That won't change. But I'm glad you're going to be a doctor, and I hope you'll stay in Canaan to practice medicine. You'll find a lot of people here who need you."

The chauffeur had carried Hank into his house, after first pounding on the front door. His mother hadn't even known he was gone because she'd sunk into a deep, exhausted sleep, after days and nights spent sitting up beside his bed.

"So!" Karl asked Hank now. "How soon do you think you'll go back to school?"

Hank shrugged. "In a couple days, probably. I've kept up with my work. Dorie Wunderly brought me all my books and stuff right before Christmas."

"Who's she? A girlfriend?"

"Heck no!" Hank exploded. "She's twice as big as I am. She could beat me into the ground and I could never get up, she's so big and mean."

Karl laughed, but stopped when he saw Hank's face begin to crumple.

"I don't understand!" Hank cried. "Billy was the biggest boy in our whole class, and the strongest, and he was never sick the whole time I knew him. So how come he's the one that had to die from the flu?"

For a long moment the room was silent. Only the mantel clock ticked in the Kerner front parlor, where the three of them sat—no, four, counting the baby. At the bottom of the hill, along the banks of the river, a train screamed. Each train whistle echoed the wails of anguish tearing at Hank's insides.

"Who can answer that?" Karl finally murmured.

Margie said, "Maybe God needed Billy Radish up in heaven."

Hank cried out harshly, "I need him a whole lot more than God does!"

Silence again, then Karl cleared his throat. "Speaking of need," he said, "we need to set a date for the baby's christening. I know you already baptized him, Hank, and that's a valid baptism, but—"

Margie broke in, "But we'd like a formal church ceremony, too, so the family could come. I sewed the baby a beautiful christening dress—months ago."

"Before anyone even knew she was expecting," Karl added.

Why were they acting as though they wanted Hank to approve their plans? "Uh-huh," he said.

"We've just been waiting till you were well enough," Margie continued. "So you can be his godfather."

"Really?"

"Well, sure," Karl said. "You saved the baby's life."

Margie nodded. "The doctor told me that when you wrapped him in that hot towel, that's what brought him around. He said sometimes if a newborn doesn't breathe right away, he'll hold it up close to a warm oven till it takes its first breath."

Hank stored that in his memory for future use.

Margie was reaching out, offering the baby to him. "You've never held your little nephew since you delivered him. Wouldn't you like to hold him?" she asked, laying the baby across Hank's knees. The movement made her wince because her back hadn't entirely healed from her fall.

The baby's solemn, round eyes looked up at Hank. For an instant they focused on Hank's face, and then the baby's mouth twisted in a fleeting, lopsided curve that disappeared so quickly Hank couldn't be sure it was actually what he thought it was.

"How old are babies when they start to smile?" he asked.

"Oh, about little Billy's age," Margie answered.

"Has he smiled for anyone yet?"

"No. He's a bit slower to do things because he was born a month too soon. He'll catch up. The doctor says he's a perfect baby."

It happened again—the momentary focusing of those infant eyes followed by the wobbly, primitive twist of the lips. Neither Margie nor Karl noticed it, but Hank knew what it was. Billy had smiled at him.

"How about it, Hank?" Karl asked. "You didn't say whether you wanted to be godfather. It's a big responsibility. . . . You have to teach him how to be a boy, and then how to be a man. He'll look up to you in a special way. So do you want to?"

"Sure I do!" A responsibility would fill some of the empty places in Hank's life. His first responsibility would be to find a gift for the baby's christening—a godparent was supposed to give a nicer-than-usual gift. Hank would buy something for the christening, but the real gift, the important gift, he'd hold back until little Billy got older.

Hank would keep the special gift upstairs in his room, where it lay now, wrapped in cotton, inside a square wooden box, tucked safely at the back of his desk drawer.

When his godson was able to understand what a beautiful and fragile thing it was, Hank would give him the Ukrainian Easter egg.

Photo Acknowledgments